CW01500392

SHAMISO

SHAMISO

BRIAN CHIKWAVA

CANONGATE

First published in Great Britain in 2025
by Canongate Books Ltd, 14 High Street, Edinburgh EH1 1TE

canongate.co.uk

1

Extract from 'Amelia at Apollo's Shrine' by Dambudzo Marechera from
Cemetery of Mind reproduced with the permission of the publisher,
Africa World Press, Inc.

British Library Cataloguing-in-Publication Data
A catalogue record for this book is available on
request from the British Library

ISBN 978 1 80530 127 1

Typeset in Bembo by Palimpsest Book Production Ltd,
Falkirk, Stirlingshire

Printed and bound by CPI Group (UK) Ltd, Croydon CR0 4YY

The manufacturer's authorised representative in the EU for product
safety is Authorised Rep Compliance Ltd, 71 Lower Baggot Street,
Dublin D02 P593 Ireland (arccompliance.com)

For Ayanda

For pale green the seedling children
Whom time soon grasps by the hair
And with rude force uproots into cynical light.

Dambudzo Marechera

1

Obese with grief, I discovered that 'I love you' was the best sentence ever. Nothing blunted pain as effectively as those three words.

When I met George in England, I knew I was standing at the crossroads of my past and future because I still had childhood memories to measure how far I had come. Each step forward felt like shedding old skin.

I still remembered my oversized school blazer, which fell below my knees. The headmistress could fit into my shirt, and I wore a wide-brimmed hat, vast as a marquee. If you were a teacher and bothered to lift my hat, you'd have found my eyes peering back, bright with surprise.

I had not forgotten that Jimson said you would be tagged if you couldn't run fast. Then, you'd have to find someone else to tag. He was an old man made of sadza, sweet potatoes, groundnuts and black-eyed peas. My Babamukuru.

I am still the little girl who spent a chunk of her childhood trying to find her way out of capacious clothes that I was expected to grow into. If my grasp of the world was behind everyone else's, it's because I saw it later than many.

You could say I was the last to see the blue sky. I could start the story there. But I will start here: Jimson at the borehole.

This is where people in Jimson's village come to fetch water. He overhears Shadreck casually telling others that Jimson's mother has developed a witching habit since she lost her husband. They say she walks naked into people's houses in the dead of night, sits on men's chests as they sleep, and pours potions in their mouths to put them under her spell.

Jimson takes offence, of course. Words are exchanged, and the sight of blood is demanded. He is a young man then. At the time, half of my father is still a twinkle in one of his father's testicles, which at that point are flying behind a plough far away near the border with Mozambique.

At dawn on Friday, Jimson and Shadreck take their knob-kerries to a granite hill where the first light is supposed to start what must conclude with one of them going down.

The air is dry, and Jimson is sure there will be no rains for several days. Whoever dies today will be buried in a season when the earth is parched, hard and unwilling to break.

He is confident that victory favours the wronged because they fight with intensity, courage and a magnanimous spirit that the ancestors lend the afflicted.

Jimson and Shadreck are familiar with the boys' fist-fight matches, a rite of passage for goat or cattle-herding boys. Familiar with the burning moment and pumping adrenaline.

There is always a crowd of boys squealing with excitement. That rare spectacle is here: the technique of violence.

A self-appointed referee moulds two breasts from the sand – one for you and the other for your opponent. You kick your opponent's mother's breast up into the air. The back heel for contempt. Now he has only one choice: save face by kicking your mother's breast or tuck his tail between his legs and slink away.

Jimson has seen many mothers' breasts hoofed up into the sky with abandon or fearfully or with cold disdain. He has seen just as many balls kicked up rear orifices. But this fight is on another level: someone must die or back down in abject humiliation.

Shadreck brings a small crowd of brothers and cousins to the fight. Jimson arrives with only a puppy. Fear crosses his heart: he's alone. They could all attack him. The puppy would not be spared.

The puppy has been named Mapenzi. Morons! It is custom to conduct sprawling, decades-long quarrels by giving your pets names that wind up the hated neighbours. Whenever anyone from Shadreck's family comes to borrow one thing or another, Jimson's mother never misses the opportunity to pretend to be calling Mapenzi at the top of her voice.

The fight is over in a flash. Someone bolts at the horror of the outcome. Another walks away and starts vomiting. Jimson stands there, shaken. Everyone here knows the gratification of smashing a watermelon with a knobkerrie. The satisfying crunch of the rind and flesh of a watermelon. But this is different; none of them can even imagine what it does to the head. But they know this has changed Jimson: he has taken a life. They are afraid of him.

Jimson's mother does not wait to find out what happens next: Jimson is spirited to Chimanimani district in the Eastern Highlands, where his father's brother settled.

He stays in Chimanimani for a year, waiting for his mother. She ought to have joined him by now. It's already been agreed that his mother will be taken in as a second wife by his father's brother.

But Jimson's mother has changed her mind. She sends a message: she is too old to start touching the flesh of yet another body. She has no need for a man.

Jimson becomes jumpy, unsure if he is still welcome at his uncle's home. The sound of a vehicle approaching the village throws him into acute anxiety. If it is a Land Rover, then it's terrible news. He is not confident his father's brother will not tip the police to spite his insolent mother.

Soon after, one evening Jimson sniffs the air and judges that rains are coming from Mozambique tomorrow morning. The downpour will wash his footprints away. So he vanishes.

Eleven years pass, during which Jimson travels through worlds in which you have to sleep very fast because somebody else needs the pillow. When he at last returns, my grandfather is dead. My father is ten and has not been the same since his father died. Someone made little father a box guitar from a 5-litre Olivine Cooking Oil tin can to cheer him up. It's this guitar that, a few days after arrival, Jimson takes hold of. He wants to show his young cousin how to play it, how to tickle the devil's ribs. So my father watches Jimson sat under the bloodwood tree, trying to pin the devil down for what seems like an eternity. When the devil starts to cackle, Jimson opens his mouth for the first time. His voice cracks with fervour; he is pulling a story out of his depths.

By afternoon half the village is crowded around this man, making the afternoon swarm with fierce locusts as if a famine is coming. They're amused by tales of jail floors colder than a police hound's nose. Jimson, who ran away, has returned as a masiganda, a troubadour. He flings songs like the red-hot copper slag he used to dump in Northern Rhodesia. He reels out his itinerant existence as a labourer in Mozambique when he was ready to be eaten alive by the feral dogs of Gaza Province.

Jimson is welcomed back to the village. He's theirs, they say. He's been further than any one of them will ever be.

2

My father is eighteen when the first comrades come to the village under cover of night, round up all the older boys and girls and herd them across the border to Mozambique. At the war's end, he will return to the country with other comrades and the surviving members of the group that were taken from the village.

They are new men and women at their homecoming. They speak foreign tongues, have new names and walk with the signature gait of people with a new way of looking. The confidence of the terrorist who became a liberator overnight.

Jimson is unsure what to make of my father, who speaks Mandarin now. He feels overawed by his cousin, whose return is a source of joy for the family and the village. Jimson also learned to speak Shangani, Bemba and Chewa over the years, but they're all languages of this side of the equator.

The family, aunts, uncles and assorted elders have travelled far to see my father. The black cow has been slaughtered, ancestors' blessings sought, and offerings of blood and beer poured on the earth to appease them. His mother died of pneumonia while he was away. After the rites have been performed to cleanse my father of the darkness that may follow him from the war, they take him to his mother's tomb near the cattle pen.

'What will you, comrades, do with this country now that you've inherited the problems of your former rulers?' Jimson asks my father after he has paid his respects to his mother. All formalities are over now, and everyone can settle down, swirl the calabash, take a sip of beer and pass it on.

Jimson is eager to establish that being the big shot among the comrades does not mean you can just order people around here. The comrades have one trick up their sleeves that he does not possess, he concedes: they know how to fire a gun. To kill. Still, he would not allow some of them to milk his precious cows even if his life depended on it: they haven't mastered any delicate skills.

My father says, 'People die for this kind of talk, you know?' He has acquired the volatile temperament of young men who have seen war, lost comrades or terminated friends' lives and become monsters. He has been turned inside out often; it's impossible to tell which way he is now.

'We left to find our lost country and have brought it back to you,' he continues.

Jimson laughs. 'The country has always been here. You left it, returned to it, and now say you returned with it? Did you carry it on your backs or in your pockets?'

My father's hands shake with unreleased fury. He lights a cigarette and walks away as he puffs. He has never liked that Jimson has always been able to wind him up with little effort. Nothing has changed.

My father leaves the military two years later to join the civil service. He has already met my mother, a gap-toothed ex-combatant with a malfunctioning mechanism in her head; the war smashed it. She lives for the bar and carries a brick in her bag in case a man follows her to lodgings. When he asks why she does not orgasm, she tells him to get over himself.

'If women had to orgasm to fall pregnant, there would only be a dozen Zimbabweans today. You would not even exist,' she says.

On the day he finds out she is pregnant with me, he tells her to get out of his flat in the middle of the night. There is yelling. Doors are slammed, and nosey neighbours wake up and peer through their curtains.

A week later, he calls her to say, 'But your clothes are still here?'

'You can burn them!' comes the reply.

He has played his last card. Soon he'll start telling my mother's friends that he doubts she is carrying his child because everyone knows she's a whaga. After my birth, he says I can't possibly be his because I don't have dimples in my cheeks. This is supposed to be incontrovertible evidence because no one in his family is without dimples.

Then he finds a proper woman who gives him two children in four years. The new republic is creating new people; Bantu faces are populating the boardrooms of parastatals, the top tiers of the civil service, the military and the police. And names of the cities and streets are changing from English to indigenous ones. The boys and girls of Zimbabwe, my father would say, tickled the devil's ribs with the AK-47, and now look, they were free. Zimbabwe was sweeter than the sweetest pumpkin, grandmothers were brewing milk-white beer, and the povo rejoiced.

When my father and his new bride buy a house in a formerly whites-only suburb, Jimson is initially reluctant to visit. He says the air is polluted in Harare, full of smoke, making it impossible to tell when the rain is approaching. He would be disoriented and not know how to time his return journey. Besides, he has cattle to look after. Two cows have already died because they ate plastic.

It's just the old ridiculous Jim, my father thinks. He is sure Jimson wants to be begged to visit; he's sore because my father didn't send a car to fetch him from the rural home for the wedding.

But Jimson holds a powerful position among the family elders. And my father will need him on his side on the issue of the child who is in the wild. My father already stands accused of forgetting himself, being too depraved to bring his blood out of the wilderness and back home. He must beg Jimson, who pretends to have been inconvenienced by all this but will come regardless because kinship cannot be washed away with Lifebuoy soap like dirt.

When word gets to Jimson that my mother's family sent my father a message to say my mother had fallen on hard times and now sells her body to truck drivers plying the Harare–Johannesburg route, Jimson gets the opportunity he's been waiting for. He sends a message to my father in the city: he is going to get me from wherever I am and bring me up himself if my father is not going to do the right thing. Family members start to talk, and not all agree with Jimson.

When elderly relatives gather at the rural home to resolve the quarrel and provide counsel, they take snuff to help them think through what they will hear. Their respect for Jimson is diminished because he never married, never reproduced. He is destined to be buried with a maize cob, the symbolic wife for a man who dies wifeless. But he's the most senior surviving man from my father's line, and nothing can be done about that. At least they agree with him on broader points. The consensus causes my father to walk off to the kraal as if he is going out to work himself up into a murderous fit and come back with an axe in one hand. But he never returns. Instead, he walks away to catch a bus and look for my mother's brother, who has taken custody of me.

I am already a hardy weed; I could grow through a concrete pavement when I join my father and his new family. My milk teeth are still falling out, though in the wrong order. I am told that Babamukuru Jimson wants to meet me. He is going to visit soon, but he never seems to come.

I have just graduated from primary school when a flinty old man I have never seen arrives at our house one Monday afternoon.

The man's overalls are rolled down to his hips, and I know right away from the force of his presence that he is the kind of person that adults would address respectfully as Them: ava; *va*Hombe; the considerable. Vawuya; they've come. A dirty hat is pulled low across their face, and they carry a battered suitcase.

I can tell the old man wants to come inside our house at the earliest possible opportunity. Unlike other people, they did not wait at the gate but opened it assuredly and walked straight in.

I cannot stop staring. They have a half-smoked cigarette tucked behind one ear and are older than my father, perhaps the same age as our gardener, Boniface.

I have not seen Boniface since coming back from school. There is no grown-up around. Usually, Boniface is busy pacing the garden with a spade on his shoulder.

The maid, Sabina, who often deals with strangers who roll in unannounced, has gone to TM Supermarket. She left me to look after my younger step-siblings, Samuel and Chipo.

The man puts down the suitcase and sits on a disused crate under the syringa tree by the stoep, wiping sweat beads from their forehead cratered with what could be old chickenpox scars. An intensity shines through their rheumy eyes.

They must have travelled a long distance.

Only yesterday, my stepmother turned away someone looking for gardening work. I try to say something to the man, but my speech impediment gets in the way. I muddle up my lines. Words get stuck, or I just can't reach them.

Fortunately, I now know how to spark my speech; it sputters to life after a couple of jolting false starts, and I eventually communicate to vaHombe, as respectfully as I can, that they are out of luck if they are looking for a job.

I am afraid they may say *pfutseke!* but thankfully that doesn't happen.

'I'm not looking for a job, Shamiso.'

So they know my name but will not greet me. Maybe they want to greet the grown-ups first before greeting children.

Their voice makes them sound like they carry an enormous creature inside.

Perhaps they expect to talk to my father or stepmother first; they appear to be organising their thoughts as if preparing a meticulous greeting speech so that, when the moment arrives, they can dazzle with the kind of Shona which, unlike its urban varieties, still recognises the significance of this kind of arrival.

My siblings and I gawp in wonder as they rummage in their back pocket and bring out a matchstick. They strike the match ablaze on the sole of their shoe and light a cigarette.

We withdraw to the tyre swing on a tree at the far end of the garden. We observe the old man sitting aloof from a safe distance, head in a cloud of cigarette smoke.

Sabina comes back swinging supermarket bags. Sabina has the vocabulary to probe this visitor without causing offence. She pokes, but the man spits out something in her direction; I don't know what that means, but the words sting Sabina. Now she assumes a cautious and conciliatory tone and reels out an elaborate line that is beyond our understanding.

After that, our house is irrevocably entered.

3

Babamukuru Jimson's transformation comes a month later on the day they must say goodbye.

They had not been a consistent hit with us kids despite trying to win us over. But they were still Babamukuru, vaHombe.

When they walked into our life unannounced, they spent the first weekend bribing us with fruit. They took us to every blood-orange and naartjie shrub. Babamukuru, please get me that one; Babamukuru, peel this one for me, and soon our hands were sticky-dry with citric zest.

Since then, Babamukuru had found more ways to entertain us. We had seen them pick a spade from the ground, flatten one nostril with the corner of the spade and blow their nose with terrific ferocity so that out of the other opening an almighty glob shot out and landed across the border in Zambia. We squealed with disgust and pleasure. Wanted more, and so Babamukuru would do it again and again until all the snot in their head was used up. Soon we didn't want to be touched by their hands, affection overcome by a slew of disgust.

It was fitting that when Babamukuru wanted to be accompanied on the last walk around the neighbourhood, none of us was keen. The promise of an ice lolly was not enough to bribe my stepsister, Chipo. Samuel did not want to go either, but our father took the choice out of his hands.

And so Babamukuru stepped out of the gate with my hand and Samuel's in theirs, charged with big claims of ownership. Samuel looked like a minor convict, unable to protest Babamukuru's overbearing affections. We knew we would be paraded over every square inch of the neighbourhood in an embarrassing public display of kinship. Our friends and schoolmates were going to ridicule us for ever.

The shopping centre was not far away. We walked through the vendors' market in the car park and quickly got to the ice cream vendors' end. We could already see a Lyons Maid vendor sitting on his bike, his uniform blending in with the flamboyants exploding red behind him.

When we got to him, he flung his lid open for us and stared into the middle distance silently. He had a bad eye: a blue cataract whose colour detonated as if struck by a lightning bolt. It was terrible and beautiful at the same time. But the eye's restless hooking motion scared us.

'But your ice cream cones are unrecognisable. You've packed them so tight you've flattened them,' Babamukuru Jimson complained.

'You don't have to buy them if you don't like them,' the vendor shot back.

The vendor held all the cards. Babamukuru relented and let Samuel and I pick the least flattened of the ice creams.

Babamukuru was happy to spoil us; their face was lit up with satisfaction as they blew smoke from a cigarette.

'And what is the damage?' Babamukuru asked.

They did not like the number they heard.

'That will leave me unable to afford cigarettes for the rest of the year, sahwira.' Babamukuru Jimson invoked sahwira-ship, hoping to open up a friendly negotiation.

'I'm not your sahwira. I will not be buttered up like that,' said the man.

'That's not how a proper person speaks to others,' Babamukuru Jimson replied, hands open in a conciliatory gesture. 'Are things okay at home, sahwira?'

'I told you I'm not your sahwira.'

'Fine. But I'm not paying full price for these things that look like a dozen chicken buses ran over them.'

Now Babamukuru Jimson goes through all trouser pockets, emptying everything, which is only about half the amount due. 'That's all I have.'

The ice cream man spits onto the tarmac and straightens his spine on the saddle. He stares into the distance, and when he has composed himself, he strikes a hand-on-hip pose to address Babamukuru in the kind of sotto voce tones reserved for an idiot.

'Let me explain this to you. Where I work, my white people count these things. Then they set strict prices. Do you want me to repeat that slowly for you?'

Babamukuru, stung by the vendor's contempt, attempts to reach for the voice that will inform this vendor that they are talking to them: vaHombe; ngumbangumba who is greater than the flesh and bones that the man is looking at.

But Babamukuru is already upset; the spirit they need is already slipping away. Giving up, they toss all their dignity up into the air as if it's a restrictive scarf and announce: 'My name is Jimson. Imagine going six feet under for ice cream! And it's not even yours. Not even your mother's!'

By the time the vendor's mother's privates get a mention, whatever remained of Babamukuru has been supplanted by a bare and basic Jimson, stubborn as a donkey. This is not *ava*. Not Them. There is always a drunk layabout here every day shouting, yelling at someone in this manner.

'We all have to make ends meet,' the man says, thrusting his head theatrically. 'Some of us are the way we are because we must walk from one end of the city to another. Or else you get home and suffer the ignominy of watching the cat getting accustomed to curling up on the stove. Do you understand?'

'Aiwa!' Jimson decides. No, he doesn't want to understand now. 'I'm not interested in false talk when children here have suffered a traumatic loss of pleasure from ice cream deformity. Even the enjoyment of the ice cream will be deformed!'

Jimson also takes offence at the man letting spittle fly as he speaks. 'It's all over the sky; people will soon start to see a rainbow if you don't stop.'

The Lyons Maid man leaps off his bike and snatches our half-eaten ice creams. He hails a police officer who dawdles towards us, sweating under his heavy tunic.

The officer listens to the complaint with dubious attention.

He inspects the remains of the ice cream with his constabulary eye, glances at his watch, and decides he is off duty now. Jimson roars with diabolical laughter. He instructs the ice cream vendor to follow him if he wants his money. The man has no choice but to follow as Jimson leisurely saunters to the bottle store. The ice cream vendor has the look of a broken man.

On the bottle store verandah is a noisy crowd of table-football enthusiasts. A knife-edge duel is on, and two men are bent over the table in maximum concentration. One of them will lose what he cannot afford to lose.

As soon as the game ends, Jimson slams the deck with a handful of coins. His gesture is met with a wary silence. People run their eyes over him, appraising.

A man emboldened by drink steps forward and places his bet down as someone warns him that table-football nonpareils can walk out of nowhere and even be as old as this sekuru.

Jimson takes his position. Samuel and I exchange bright-faced looks: we have never been so proud. He is every inch a table-football legend to whom a game is an inconvenient formality because he's only here to take money from a fool. If this man had any sense, he would save himself plenty of trouble by handing over a fraction of his daily earnings.

The game is over in a flash, and the crowd doubles up with laughter. Everyone now wants a shot at playing Jimson. Twenty-dollar bills are being waved in the air, and Jimson is already trying to explain to the Lyons Maid man that he was dangerous at this game back in the day. He feels compelled to whip out his Post Office Savings Bank book to assure the ice cream man that he has a lot of money.

'Follow me if you want your money, Mr Lyons Maid,' Jimson commands, this time setting foot towards home.

A tone of genuine anger is creeping into the ice cream man's voice; he keeps tripping on the broken pavement; he can't maintain his poise. Still, he pushes his bicycle along. By the time we get home, the ice cream man has lost the ability to speak; he's livid and maintains a homicidal silence under the syringa tree as Jimson disappears into the house.

It would have ended well had the vendor not handed back $4.99 worth of coins instead of a $5 note as change. Breaking up a whole banknote for the sake of one cent!

'Stupicide! Bloody idiot! Plastic eater!' Jimson's veins bulge out of his neck. He wants to feel the man's collar.

My father steps in only to be laughed at by Jimson. 'You're not qualified to touch me, you. Show respect!'

'Behave like an elder; do not embarrass us. Neighbours are looking.'

'You can't tell me what is wrong and what is right. You have put on the white man's soiled undergarments, assumed his ways and feel no shame about having a garden boy who is old enough to be your father. You can't tell me anything.'

Boniface, the gardener, walks away. Now it's Jimson and my father's turn to seize each other's collars.

Jimson's elbow use quickly demonstrates how a new idea dumbfounds the unprepared. My father springs off the ground as if he wants us to believe nothing happened. He is dazed, but it's not clear if this is because of the blow or because

18

the possibility that a civilian could be better at combat than a comrade is offensive.

Now he charges. Explosively. Same mistake, same outcome. Clean.

'You'd be dead if this was real,' Jimson goads my father.

My father throws himself at Jimson again recklessly. It doesn't matter because luck is on his side this time: they lock arms. He has been trying to get into this position: I have watched enough judo to know. They test each other's strength. Father's attempts to sweep Jimson's feet off the ground are useless against an opponent with cat-like agility.

Then Jimson loses his footing, is thrown down with savage force, hits the earth with his shoulder and a collarbone flicks out of him like a penknife.

4

He did not intend to return to the rural home anyway, Babamukuru Jimson announced a week after his fracture. The indignity of saying he had nowhere to go had stopped him from speaking up earlier. There was nothing to return to since the drought wiped out most of the livestock; there was neither water nor food out there.

His arm was in a sling. The fracture required surgery, and my father was on a chair by Babamukuru Jimson's bed. They were absorbed in conversation and didn't acknowledge me when I walked in with Babamukuru's lunch.

Chamu, son of a deceased aunt who shared custodianship of the rural home with Babamukuru Jimson, rushed to marry into the neighbouring family while his mother's blood was still warm in the grave. Chamu's wife's family tipped the authorities during the war that my father was a guerrilla, resulting in my grandfather being jailed. Now, the family had talked Chamu into paying extortionately to settle the roora and he had surrendered what remained of the family's livestock.

'And you've said nothing about this all this time?' My father stubbed out a cigarette.

'I wrote a letter to you, asking all of you people to come over to put our heads together, and heard nothing. I wrote a letter to mai-Rutendo, I heard nothing back. I wrote a letter to Zebedia and got nothing back. I wrote a letter to Tafirenyika, and he said he was too busy. Not one of you can say I didn't tell them. What was I supposed to do about Chamu on my own?'

A year later, we would learn that Chamu and his new wife had started a new life in a squatter camp in Epworth, just outside the city. No one was left kumusha; we were now like Malawian migrants who don't have rural homes in this country. At least they had theirs in Malawi.

'We are now as good as imaginary people,' Babamukuru said when he heard about Chamu and the dereliction of the rural home.

'It's still home,' my father insisted. 'It does not stop being home just because there's no one there.' He looked humiliated; he was the only family member who could have done something to save the home. Chipo, Samuel and I must not mention this to our friends, or we'd be regarded as a lightweight family, rootless people without any honour.

Babamukuru Jimson had no wish to see Chamu and his wife.

'They might kill me in their hovel and sell my body parts,' he said.

★

When my father and the rest of the family travelled to Gweru for a long weekend, I was left with Jimson, Sabina and Boniface. Babamukuru Jimson, who had almost completely recovered now except for occasional spasms in his shoulder, said I should slip into my shoes and accompany him to Mbare.

We spent the day traipsing all Mbare market, looking for pink rubber bands. He wanted to make a slingshot, and pink rubber bands from aircraft wheels were better than the standard red variety from the tube of a car's wheels.

I was unsure what the slingshot was for but stopped thinking about it when Babamukuru Jimson bought me a pendant. It was a reward for accompanying him, he said.

The pendant was a stone carving of Nyami Nyami, the River God, the spirit snake. My first instinct was fear that one day I would break it. It looked fragile, a needle of stone with Nyami Nyami's serpentine body coiled up and gathered at the top, where instead of a snake's head, a fierce fish's head sprung out bearing sharp teeth. It was surprisingly heavy. I wore it straight away.

A snake with a fish's head. It was a strange form, as if all life forms were connected and fluid in their existence. No one had ever given me anything like this before.

I was glowing inside but could not help suspect that the reason Jimson wanted a slingshot was Boniface, the gardener. Boniface committed the cardinal sin of thinking himself superior to rural folk. Sometimes he spoke about the city council needing to limit the number of black people who bought houses in these suburbs. He had had enough of this or that pretender from the townships who buys a big house in the western suburbs and can't tell goldfish and flower apart, but then his uncles and aunts start visiting and think they can order servants around! Tsk!

Boniface had made it clear to Jimson that he was not going to tolerate relatives putting on airs when he had worked for white people for decades without being treated with such contempt. If the new overlords had any decency, they would pay him an extra wage to hold their hand through the white lifestyle they were so desperate to have.

It was already dark when Jimson and I caught a commuter omnibus back home, having found the elusive pink rubber bands.

In the morning, Jimson finished making his slingshot. It was a strange-looking object, chunky, robust and sinister. Jimson asked me to give it a try. It was harder to pull than the regular ones. Frightened of slingshots because a boy from school accidentally shot into his little brother's eye, I hastily handed it back to Jimson.

Jimson grabbed the lone armchair from the verandah and sat under the syringa tree, which still had berries. Go-away birds were noisily feeding up there.

By midday, Jimson had single-handedly shifted the neighbourhood's ecological equilibria, depleting an entire population of go-away birds. The foolish birds kept coming, maybe because this was one of the few syringa trees still in fruit.

Under the tree, the ground was carpeted grey with the birds' corpses. Whenever one started flapping about in its death throes, Jimson would show me how to snap the neck and put it out of its misery.

I was relieved the slingshot was not for shooting Boniface, but I feared what he was going to do when he returned to find the neighbourhood plunged into silence and the go-away bird population down to single digits. I did not want to let that bother me and buried my anxiety in snapping my way through bird necks with the enthusiasm of a criminal apprentice.

Boniface found us standing by the braai stand in the afternoon, with scores of birds sizzling over the coals.

'I just sat there and went ri-ki-ta ri-ki-ta ri-ki-ta, and the birds dropped one by one. Have you ever seen a better shooter?' Jimson asked.

Here, Boniface calls Sabina, who has been in the house all the time. When Sabina sees the absurdity of what has happened, she unravels in a fit of laughter. It's not the reaction Boniface is looking for. He says he cannot stick around and be implicated in this madness. He does not even wish to give a witness statement to the police because he wants to stay well out of it.

We watch his angular frame march to the boys' khaya. He returns with a bag over his shoulder and heads off to spend the weekend with his extended family in Norton.

In the morning, Jimson delegates me the task of finding a pencil, paper and rubber. He says we need to be on top of our numbers once we get to musika.

He irons his brown trousers so that the creases are straight and achingly sharp: flies that dare land on them will be cut in half and fall to the ground.

By mid-morning, we have set up at the musika by the shopping centre. I have never done this before and I'm

24

looking forward to talking to lots of people. I'm beginning to learn to focus in a specific way that does not trigger brain circuits that activate my speech impediment.

Our roast birds are out on display on a wire rack, and Jimson has already determined that he will not let his birds be bought by the povo but by proper people. He holds his long wire fork uncompromisingly. He did not iron his trousers to impress layabouts pointing their broke fingers at his birds. Nix!

The sort of buyer that Jimson wishes for tends to sweep into the shopping centre car park in a German car, hop out and stride into Bon Marché. Later, they emerge trailed by supermarket assistants pushing groaning trolleys, drop into the driver's seat and drive off without ever looking in our direction.

Jimson is adamant he won't demean himself by chasing after anyone. Already there has been a dispute over the spot where we set up. The vendors cannot hide their resentment. The bad-tempered exchange between Jimson and everyone has killed any possibility of goodwill. We claimed a spot reserved for a worshipful somebody still on his knees in a church somewhere in the city centre.

A big-boned woman wearing a black doek and swaying layers inches over to Jimson's birds. Jimson suspects she is only here to spy on prices. At least the woman does not commit the sin of pointing at the birds – that always triggers an ir-rational response from Jimson. Still, the woman takes her time, inspecting in silence before wandering off to the next vendor.

Later, when she returns to ask Jimson the going rate for the birds, he answers, 'Forgive me, mother of children. People must be well scrubbed and in their Sunday best before I can reveal my prices. Not when you have cracked heels that can shelter a black mamba.'

The woman walks away without even responding. Her unhurried, deliberate gait is that of someone who is too aware that Jimson has already done enough to antagonise the vending ranks. She's going to bide her time.

She stops for a brief conversation with a man who has just arrived with hands in pockets, impudent head held high in the air.

'I hear there is a wonder here who has quite a mouth,' the man says as the woman walks away. He's casting his gaze around and obviously knows everyone here.

Yes, that is the situation here, someone shouted. 'That's the sitchaz!'

A breastfeeding woman beside us plunges her neck into her shoulders like a winter dove on a wire. She looks the other way to avoid us catching her eye. Nasty things have started flying in the air, and vendors on three sides around us are talking over our heads. One gurgles and spits a throatful of insults, another baits with sarcasm, and a third one goads Jimson with extravagant laughter.

'Plastic eaters doing the usual stupicide!' Jimson mumbles. We will be reduced to a bloodstain on the tarmac if he loses his cool.

Then appears Jimson's bête noire: the Lyons Maid ice cream vendor. Jimson is delighted to see the man. The last time they crossed paths, it was not a happy episode.

This time Jimson extends the conciliatory offer of a free roast bird to the man, but it is rejected. The ice cream man is still angry.

Jimson points his eyes to the ground. The paved surface is torn at this end, and there are a few loose concrete blocks; Jimson now grabs a couple and places them on the edge of his rack of birds.

He warns the Lyons Maid man that he once kicked a big man's rear orifice and the man became mentally deranged on the spot. The Lyons Maid man takes it like his mother's breast has been kicked into high noon. He's ready to put on a show.

'This little old man standing with you is unforgivable,' he addresses me now. I do not know what to say. People are whistling, impatient to witness an outburst of violence.

Jimson and I start gathering our things because the man whose spot we claimed has arrived. We move there and then over there. Soon the vendors are making us hop from one spot to another until the whole thing is a sport for them. If we don't want violence, this is one way for the crowd to discharge its pent-up anger. No sooner do we set up than we are moved on again.

When Jimson finally stands unrecognisably vanquished, the doek woman he insulted emerges and buys everything in bulk at a discount she has dictated. She even follows us home and cleans up all the remaining stock.

On Monday morning, Sabina finds the kitchen and pantry transformed into one almighty sugar ants' nest, thanks to Jimson's aborted attempts at making fudge for me.

Sabina rouses us from our beds and throws us out into the garden, where we must find our place in the hierarchies of flora and fauna.

'Nyami Nyami suits you,' Babamukuru Jimson says, throwing an arm around my shoulders for the first time. I should be anxious about what my parents say about my involvement with Babamukuru's delinquency. Instead I feel balanced, less like a sprat in stormy waters and more like the serpentine river god who calms turbid Zambezi waters with the curl of their tail. The sense of being off-balance that appeared in me on the day I was brought here and my stepmother screamed *kwete mumba mangu* at my father, is gone.

Kwete mumba mangu. Not in my house!

We wander around the garden and briefly stand in the open air, observing an aircraft. It was up in the clear morning sky but has vanished without a trace and no vapour trail. I missed the moment, tried to keep my eyes peeled to the pinpoint when the jet would dissolve into nothingness, but I could not. The sun caught its side and turned it bronze. The aircraft lingered over the horizon as it diminished to a dot. Then it was gone. One moment it was there, and the next moment it was not.

5

In the years following the bird massacre I became aware of myself breathing because it was the only way I knew how to make Nyami Nyami gather and coil inside me.

Each year was supposed to be a progressively smaller fraction of the length of time I'd been alive so that time moved faster, but I felt as if everything moved in slow motion. As if we lived at the bottom of a sea of treacle, and every movement was tenfold slower. Sometimes dust motes floated motionless in shards of sun poking in through my window, and when a flying insect looped through the air, I could almost see its flight path ripping through space.

Babamukuru Jimson was never far away, but I no longer needed him to be there for me to stand up to my stepmother. As long as I could feel him through the pendant, I could hold on to my inner stillness.

I was always afraid of my father, but fearful in a different way from how I feared my stepmother, who did not hesitate to use her hands.

I had witnessed Babamukuru strike an unlikely friendship with Farai from next door. Farai had just completed his postgrad at the university and was waiting to go to Scotland for further studies. When he was around, he came to our house to spend time with Babamukuru in the garden.

One Saturday afternoon, when Farai got up to return home, Babamukuru Jimson walked him to the gate. I liked Farai and wanted to tag along as usual.

We had only just reached the gate when my stepmother emerged from the house calling for me. She wanted me to dash off to the shops to get fresh milk and was already waiting on the stoep, holding a $10 note.

'I'm coming just now. We are only walking Farai to his gate,' I said.

'No. Now. I don't like to be kept waiting!'

'Only two minutes?'

So she walked over to us and, cold and clinical, scattered my senses across the sky with a swift backhander.

I find I am less afraid of her as an assault progresses. Less of a shrinking flower and insolently bold. Sometimes for that, you receive a bonus smack. You've got to keep rising because people are terrified of things that can't be killed and yet aren't attacking; they're forced to consider the possibility they've misunderstood something big about life. It helps if you've watched someone eating while you rub an empty stomach, because that's where you learn to separate and be double. How to fly away from yourself. You may not always find your way back home and are tossed, spun dizzy, and buffeted every which way by the quiet storms inside. But through spirit snake, you always arrive home at the flat calm clear blue waters that no one can rock. My stepmother cannot touch me.

Jimson and Farai try to help me along. Jimson takes my hand and says, 'On TV, the news is all Palestinians' wails. There is no need to crowd the air with more sorrow.'

He and Farai walk me to the shops to buy the required milk, and on the way, we come across a family of brown toads. Jimson crouches down to stroke one of them with a straw, and it issues a meow, puffs up and secretes its milky bufotoxins.

★

I saw my stepmother giving Babamukuru Jimson a wad of banknotes for his labour in the garden one afternoon and overnight became ashamed of my parents and Jimson.

I noticed there were periods now when I could not feel my Nyami Nyami on my chest, and that always made me feel vulnerable.

They knew what they were doing was not right because Jimson had initially protested, saying, 'That's not done! Accepting money from a relative's hand for work brings bad luck.'

My stepmother said the money was a contribution towards Babamukuru Jimson's cigarettes, and Jimson took a deep breath, puffed his cheeks out in contemplation and cracked up.

'This kind of generosity is calculated to ruin my lungs, isn't it?' he laughed. 'You must wish me dead.'

My stepmother laughed. They laughed nervously, conspiratorially, and the strangeness of what I'd witnessed stuck in my gut as if I'd swallowed a knife.

A few weeks later, when Jimson came to the kitchen for lunch, he was surprised by Sabina insisting on handing him his food through the kitchen window. She said she was only doing what she was instructed to do. And, of course, she agreed with my stepmother because Babamukuru's boots always brought mud and dirt into the kitchen.

'And anyway, Boniface never once objected to receiving his lunch through the window, did he?' Sabina asked.

'But am I Boniface?'

Jimson took the plate and went to sit on the verandah. He ate in silence. Boniface was long retired, so Jimson could not have misunderstood what was happening. Boniface was gone, and the boy's khaya at the far end of the garden was vacant.

I return from school one day to find that Babamukuru has moved all his belongings into the boy's khaya. He has been told to make himself comfortable there.

Soon I start seeing Jimson lying under the syringa tree like a corpse every afternoon. I have seen variations of this native son in stupendous sleep on grain bags on a scotch cart under some tree. Listlessly waiting for the mill operator to return from the other side of the vastness of the rural world.

Once in a while, Jimson gets up and puts a foot on a garden fork. Then he stares blankly into space. Soon he's talking to the shadows around him.

Jimson seems almost reconciled to his fate at the end of the month. He is good at it: moving on. I recall him once saying that you have to be like that if you want to come out of worlds where you have to sleep very fast so that someone else can use the pillow.

After school, I spend my afternoons with him. He is terminally distracted, as if he has lost the capacity to inhabit the present moment fully. I repeat every question, and he answers twice every time. Sometimes I tell him he has already answered the question. Sometimes I let him be.

Then my stepmother sees the maid Sabina serving Jimson his traditional afternoon tea.

'You ought to stop creating extra work for yourself,' my stepmother tells Sabina. 'Babamukuru is more than capable of making tea for himself. Making tea is one of his hidden talents. He's too modest to flaunt it. Is that not so, Babamukuru Jimson?'

Jimson raises a hand uncertainly and morphs into a pupil ambushed by a teacher. His mouth takes on a myriad of shapes but produces no sound. Then he starts nodding excessively. I loathe him surrendering his dignity in this pathetic way.

'Yes, I can make tea,' he concedes. He tries to negotiate deferral of the new regime, but my stepmother's polite laughter is the best he gets. He is sitting bolt upright on his chair. He is going to be destroyed because he has turned himself into a weird thing here. I can't help him. I once had a Babamukuru. Now all I have is this stranger thrusting a beggar's broken smile into the afternoon sunshine. I don't even trust that he would be on my side if I tried to defend him.

Maria brightens my life when she joins my class at the beginning of the year. She and her mother have relocated to Harare from London.

Maria is funny and pretty. Her manner and her London accent inspire as much awe as inferiority in the class. No one can compete with London, and girls who taste inferiority know what hurts: she is frozen out. I'm her only friend in the class. She does not get how people can be in awe of her one minute and nasty the next.

The first argument we have is over Nyami Nyami. I've been wearing this thing for years, but the last time I felt its weight on my chest was when I replaced the leather strap with a silver chain over a year ago. I can't even recall the last time I saw it in a mirror in front of me. But Maria notices during our walk home, after school.

She says she has seen these sold on every street corner. 'They're dirt cheap,' she says, and I know she doesn't mean that in a horrible way. They're popular with souvenir-buying tourists; I don't understand how she can be so dismissive of the tastes of tourists from Europe, so I'm unable to tease her about that. But when she says Nyami Nyami is a she, I laugh.

'What's so funny about that?' she says.

'I've never thought about Nyami Nyami as she.'

'So Nyami Nyami is a he?'

'I've never thought that way either. There are no gender pronouns in Shona.'

'Kind of makes sense since people believe in spirits in this country.'

'I don't understand,' I laugh. Maria's foreignness is endearing; she can hardly string a sentence in Shona and sometimes comes up with mad ideas.

'In a land of spirits the people would be cursed if they started using gender pronouns, wouldn't they?'

'Why?'

'The spirits are genderless. No?'

'Is that really true?'

'You just said Nyami Nyami has no gender.'

I give it a moment's thought and laugh. 'Okay, you win this one! For now!'

I'm surprised and flattered in June when, without warning, Maria brings her quivering little breasts and peach thighs untouched by the sun to our house.

When she asks me who the old man is, I say, 'Ah, it's only the garden boy. His name is Jimson.' I am ashamed of being seen with him. I wish he'd stop appearing at my school events in overalls. But he keeps doing it, coming to inter-house athletics competitions, the swimming gala and even to parents' day. Always lost, always impossible to tell apart from the groundsmen.

'Iwe, Shamiso!' he shouts, turning his head towards us. His garden fork falls from his hand, and he starts marching towards us.

I'm not going to listen. I have an irrational urge to destroy Jimson. I turn to the sky and laugh with impudence, wheeling away, spinning, arms outspread and determined to disorient myself with whirling motion. I do not want to hear him. I am beyond reach; the sky is circling blue above. I feel blood gathering and swelling my fingertips as I spin faster and beyond the old man's reach. Faster and faster, as if I intended to helicopter up into the sky.

Babamukuru Jimson watches in disbelief as I spin my way out of the gate.

'Why are you being so childish?' Maria asks, following me.

Two days later, Babamukuru has packed their bags and gone after so many years.

A week later, we learn that they have stepped out of this world by way of a rope.

6

One of the mourners sings about the orphan's cry on the day of its mother's death. People weep. I keep my distance. I avoid situations that will oblige me to talk.

This year, I discovered that leaning towards singing as I speak can erase my stutter. I do not feel confident speaking in that manner here, or Jimson's spirit may accuse me of self-indulgent affectation. He said I'd become a mu-salad, a salad person. The Africans who bought houses in previously whites-only suburbs sent their children to formerly white schools, and now their children struggle to speak Shona; they're not real people of the soil and have caught the imaginary illnesses of the minds of white people who are too liberal.

At night I'm unable to sleep. I'm afraid to fall asleep. I'm not sure if I am asleep or awake. I lie flat on an operating table when I lock eyes with the surgeon, whose eyes look familiar behind the surgical mask. But I can't put a name to the face. When the surgeon plunges a pair of tweezers into my ear and pulls out a spider, its leg snaps. The creature shoots off and criss-crosses my face in a blind panic before disappearing up my nose: I swallow it and start to separate. I break out of my sleep with a scream.

After the funeral, one morning, I go to the boy's khaya and gather all the wood carvings Babamukuru made since our neighbour Farai talked him into trying his hand at crafts and art. I carved some of these pieces when Babamukuru wanted me to be his apprentice two years ago. But I can no longer tell which piece was carved by me and which by him. I enjoyed using the adze, I realise. Chopping away. Getting lost in the sound and motion. I could go on and on until the appearance of blisters on my hands.

The stone pieces are too big, too heavy, and tower above my head, mute and strange. I can't move these.

I use my pocket money savings to hire a Peugeot 404 station wagon taxi to transport the carvings to the city centre. I fill up the boot and rear seat right up to the roof and make myself comfortable in the decomposing upholstery of the front passenger seat. The driver has already exhausted his quota of small talk for the day. We don't speak.

He takes me to the Harare Gardens, parks his vehicle by the entrance, and, surprisingly, helps me offload the pieces onto the pavement. I had not thought about how I would carry the carvings into the gardens, where most vendors are. So I spread them over the pavement. The driver surprises me with a sudden generosity of spirit, leaping into the role of the town crier. I watch him going about in the gardens announcing that people can come and help themselves. 'All free!'

I'm superstitious and don't want to invite bad luck. I will not sell the pieces. The pieces are all animal forms. Babamukuru mostly carved totem animals. The buffalo, the elephant, the baboon, the antelope, the bird, the fish – he could always start talking to a random stranger on the street and discover or make up some kind of kinship. The baboon carving, his totem, is chunky, unpolished, not made to tourist tastes like other pieces.

The carvings fly away quick. I'm relieved. I leave Harare Gardens and walk home. I need to walk because something tells me that if I can get my body tired, I might be able to reboot myself. I gave up carving with Babamukuru because I thought carving was not for girls. Maybe my carvings were not good, and Babamukuru threw them away. Or perhaps they are good. Good as Babamukuru's pieces, but that's not plausible.

I visit Babamukuru's grave in Warren Hills Cemetery regularly until the end of the year, and then I stop because I feel nothing. I know I'm not supposed to feel this way. I'm supposed to feel the presence of his remains at the bottom of the grave, but a water drain by the road also makes me feel this way. Maybe it's because they should not have been buried at Warren Hills but kumusha, our rural home. But there was no one there any more.

I don't know of any family like mine. We are the last people.

The last time I visit the grave, I go to Maria's house, and she gives me an overlong hug in their sitting room. I'm cold inside, and that bothers Maria. She really, really wants to make me feel loved. Squeeze me. Shake me.

Caress my cheek. Kiss me. I don't feel worthy of any connection.

When Maria's mother walks into the room, she says, 'This nonsense happens to other people's daughters, not mine!'

'Does this Shamiso not have a home?' she shouts at Maria.

'No.'

'No?'

'Yes, she does.'

'So what is Shamiso doing here, and why are you aiming so low?'

'Nothing.'

'Nothing?'

'Leave us alone!' says Maria, earning herself a smack.

Maria's mother calls Josphat, their gardener. He comes running from the back of the house, applies a bandit's grip on my arm and drags me towards the gate where he shoves me out. I don't care.

When I get home, I look for my Nyami Nyami pendant. I need to find my centre. I long stopped wearing the fish-headed snake but need it now. Inside I feel I'm about to be trapped, though I don't understand how and by what. I'll be trapped if I lose my inner flow: then I will turn into a lump of rock.

It should be in the top drawer in my room, but it's not there. It must be somewhere. I turn my room upside down but find nothing.

My siblings, Samuel and Chipo – one of them must know. I turn everything in their rooms upside down too. At first, they are surprised, confused, and then cross. But soon they're scared of me. I see it in their eyes. How can no one know where my Nyami Nyami is?

There's nothing in my parents' room either. I'm separated without a way back to myself.

I go to bed and my eyeballs seem to roll and point my pupils into my skull. By morning, when I wake up, I have walked over 75 kilometres out of Harare and all the way to Marondera where it is raining, and I must catch a chicken bus to the Chimanimani Mountains where ancestor spirits roam.

I arrive after midday, and as soon as I jump off the bus, it begins to drizzle again. I start the journey up the mountain.

I become aware of myself again when the rain stops. I'm way up at a great altitude, and the air still tastes like lightning from a couple of hours before. I am surrounded by mountains in every direction. The long trek has cooked me, and my flesh wills to fall off my bones.

I take my shoes off so I can feel mud between my toes, know how heavy I am from the cut of jagged rocks under my naked feet. I need to know when I have arrived at the site of my rendezvous with my ancestors. There must be a sign.

I realise I've never been told how to meet this hour. At first, I am unsure if I am going through the right experience. I could be experiencing something entirely different from what I expected.

My shoelaces went missing way back. I don't remember when and where. I have had to strip bark fibre off a nearby bush, tie the shoes together and hang them at the top end of my forked walking stick.

I march up the mountain, determined to feel everything under my feet. As the night falls, I find a rock and plonk myself down with all my weight. I must gather strength for the final push to the top.

I get up and march onwards into darkness. The breeze carries a song to which I offer no resistance. Its gyre populates with voices as it tightens and edges me closer to the centre. I want it to disappear me. I adjust my stride so that it falls in with the beat. Bit by bit, beat by beat, I realise I have transferred the entire song to limb and walking stick in no time and am now lost in the rhythmic calm of my stride and voice. I'm beyond the reach of any stammer.

Sometimes a twig snapping under my foot triggers the disintegration of a family of long-tailed shrikes. They scatter in all directions, flying backwards across the sky as they laugh and vanish. And my wristwatch's hands spin in opposite directions.

By midnight I stand barefoot on the mountain peak. The rain started and stopped again. It has taken all day and evening to trek up here.

My father's place of birth is not more than 20 kilometres away. If I had the eyes of a bird of prey, I'd be able to see the remains of the village from where I am. Below me, the cliff is a vast silent facade of vertigo-inducing height, even at nighttime. I can end it here, but I hear inside me the spirit snake's voice saying, I have a choice. I can die with my choice or live with it.

'Yes?' I say aloud, and my voice bounces off rock and returns to me as if from another realm.

For the first time, I allow myself to be angry with Jimson.

The red earth's mineral aroma is blowing up from below and up to this altitude. I hold tight onto my stick and tumble down the slopes. There is not much scree on this side of the mountain. I can descend fast. This is my choice.

Halfway down, I find myself on a moonlight-dappled path in a thick wood. I march under the knitted canopies and lose sight of the mountain's peak and sky.

The path tears up into three. The undergrowth rustles, and a cricket starts abruptly; I do not flinch when its sonic drill goes through my heart. I let it pass through me and continue. This too is a choice.

My feet walk in one world while my head remains in another. When the earth has spun half a right angle on its axis, I am under the sidereal gaze of the firmament. I feel fat in my head as if the tumid, sleeping-elephant shape of the mountain range is inside me. Some moments I wobble, thinking about what kind of a person my choices will turn me into, but I must keep moving. I know I must keep flying. That too is a choice.

I am out of the valley at the sun's first appearance on the mountaintops. The air is icy cold, and the sky has fallen so low I can touch it if I climb a tall tree. A parhelion in the eastern horizon.

In the afternoon, I arrive in Harare on the back of a communal farmer's pick-up truck. Sat with a goat that keeps looking me in the eye with astonishment, recognition or both.

I climb out of the truck at the railway station and wish the goat well. Then I march into the city.

The sun splinters in the sky and falls on my face in shards. I have no money, so instead of going to the Rezende Street terminus to catch a bus, I'll have to walk.

I pick my way through First Street, through street kids with broken smiles and beggars splattered on the pavements. I feel like a rumour quietly passing through the streets and emerging at the other end of Harare Gardens.

I'm in the Avenues area now. Seemingly pleasant and leafy by day, by night, the place turns into something of a red-light district.

It will take me an hour to walk home. I'm depleted and envy the people I see squashed into Peugeot 404 station wagons as they roar past me every few minutes. Bodies crammed in, pug-faced on the rear window, dangling legs beneath a half-shut boot.

7

My father says I've lost my mind because I've become absorbed in the ways of my friends, ma-salad. This has the odd effect of making me pity him for the first time. He doesn't know his daughter, neither does he know how to go about understanding her. I have gone from being possessed by a crazy spirit from my mother's people to being mu-salad within a week.

I will not contest his suggestion that I lack contact with real life or that some things must be ripped out of me before it's too late. He has a clear path: boarding school. It's a real school with rooted people, not ma-salad. He knows all the great schools that produced our national heroes. Discipline and rigour – that will iron out the kinks inside me. Then I'll get my act together there, study hard, pass and go on to study medicine at the university.

He won't drop me at school. Instead, he takes me to Mbare Bus Terminus and helps me load my trunk onto a bus. I'm travelling goat-class out of Harare.

Half the passengers are in uniform and heading to my new school. A bottle of Smirnoff vodka gets passed around early in the journey. I can't see anything suggesting this is national hero material.

On my arrival, the house mistress, Mrs Zhou, asks if I'm the girl who gets possessed by spirits. I can't imagine why my father said that.

'No.'

'Well, possessed or mu-salad, everything ends here.'

She's on my case, clearly. I must report my progress to her daily.

By the week's end, everyone calls me Mrs Zhou's girl: one of the lot who cannot be trusted to stay on the straight and narrow.

Groups of girls stop talking when I turn my head to look at them. Sometimes they laugh.

The fear of madness helps me pull myself together. Where I come from, mad people are dangerous and unpredictable because they're irrational. A boy on our road lost his mind and tried to pull his eyeball out. I will not lose my head; that has no good outcomes.

I can't think about escaping because I don't know what I should be fleeing. I accept without complaint the angular posture and other square and formal things that boarding school drills into people. The grind of walking the path to the classroom, the dining room and back to the dormitory colours the hours grey.

Tsungayi becomes an instant star when she ties a string to her blazer and drags it on the dirty pavement to the dining hall because the house mistress told her off for her unkempt appearance.

The sky flies high when Angela pushes a banana so deep into herself that she must be seen by a doctor. Thereafter, she achieves the rare feat of being simultaneously despised as 'Banana Girl' and envied for her self-confidence.

There's no sky left after a priest comes to warn us about the dangers of homosexuality, bringing carrots, cucumbers, bananas and other vegetables to show the girls the kind of things that corrupt us, turning us into homosexuals. He ends the session by casually crunching on a cucumber, right in front of us.

He's someone's father.

8

At Harare international airport, outside departures, my father unloads the car, hurriedly fetches a trolley and pushes my bags into the airport. They look like the porter, and I understand this is how they show affection. It's unlike the last time when they shoved me on a chicken bus and sent me to boarding school.

Of course, they're disappointed I'm not going to study medicine. I'm over eighteen now and can vote. I can choose. They're not thrilled I made a successful application for a scholarship. Perhaps they're ashamed that many changes in my life are happening without their say. But it's not my fault that my first Nyami Nyami carving won the art competition at school and came third in the National Gallery Schools Competition. My art teacher said that your chances are high when you apply for an undergraduate scholarship with such a record.

I'm a Nestlé Baby Milk baby. I'm supposed to be underdeveloped; the brain circuit that only a mother's nipple ignites never flickered to life.

After I check in, we have nothing to say to each other. My father is not a father who gives or receives hugs. They proffer their hand but quickly realise how ludicrous that looks. So they just stand there, flailing in awkwardness. I half-expect them to laugh, but that's not their way. I wish Chipo and Samuel were here, but it's a day flight and they're at school.

'Flying during daytime is wonderful because you can see what you're flying over,' my father says as they pivot on their heel and wave goodbye. How odd that they can make fat cooks, gratifying little things. Fat cooks are the only things I've ever seen them make in the kitchen because my stepmother can't make them like their mother did.

After boarding I go straight to my seat. It's not a window seat, but I can see the clear blue sky. It has been years since I saw a star in daylight. I now know that sometimes if you search the sky and focus well, it is possible to see a star or two, even at midday. They could be satellites, but I see three blinking points in the sky.

Gabriel and I miss each other at the arrivals exit at Gatwick airport. A tannoy announcement is made for me to meet them by the info desk. I hear it but fail to associate myself with my name because I have sensory overload.

I'm still inside a cubicle in the toilets with a speaker right over my head when I finally realise the announcement is meant for me.

Gabriel is a dark-as-a-blueberry man with the shabby look of a drunk headmaster in a queue at the post office. They're waiting for me by the info desk. I know they are on the

Birchenough Trust scholarship awards committee. You don't get that far if you can't count very high.

Gabriel and their wife offered to house me because my scholarship award came through late when campus rooms had already been allocated.

'How was your flight?'

'Good.'

'Good.'

They do all the talking as we make our way to the car park.

It's already dark outside. We catch the shuttle to the car park, and I am surprised that Gabriel drives an old purple VW Beetle; it looks rather frivolous for them.

I stare out of the window, taking in England as they drive us out of the airport. I have nothing much to hold a conversation about. I also do not know how to read Gabriel.

As we slip onto the motorway, other roads and roundabouts fly towards us at angles. Multiple heights and chevrons on the tarmac transform into arrows flying backwards. Even the birds momentarily seem to fly in reverse across the evening sky.

The sight of a passenger train gliding across the evening sparks release in my stomach. It is as if this is the sign I need to remember that I am finally far away from . . . I don't know what.

At a BP service station, Gabriel stops to fill up the tank and returns to the car with two bottles of water, joking about how the soul cannot travel faster than the speed of a donkey, and that means that my soul is likely still trying to find its way out of Harare.

9

In the morning I looked out of the window and saw England in daylight for the first time. I could see the sea in the distance.

Gabriel took me to the campus in the morning, shepherded me through the university administrative maze, smoothing over administrative knots at the registration office. I felt looked after and was glad I didn't have to do any heavy lifting in an unfamiliar environment.

Gabriel wished me luck and said I should not freak out but that if I do, I must remember that everyone else is freaking out too.

What remained to be done to complete my registration was simple and straightforward. But something happened to the computer in front of the woman serving me.

'No, thanks,' the woman said curtly when I offered to help. She did not believe I could help her. I felt weird because I had never been this impulsive: leaping to someone's aid.

I watched the woman repeatedly try to restart the machine without joy. She called IT but seemed unhappy with what she heard from the other end.

'I can't wait that long!' She sighed and hung up.

Nearly an hour later, when the computer had been fixed and my registration confirmed, one of the reception ladies took me to the lecture theatre where I found my new classmates sitting, chewing the ends of their pens, slouching or displaying varieties of inattention or boredom.

I sat through the lecture trying to get my bearings on every possible level.

I joined my classmates again at the cafeteria for lunch and noticed that cliques had already started forming.

Someone asked me where I lived.

'In the hills,' I answered and hoped there was a place in Brighton that could be called that.

On our journey from the airport yesterday I gathered that Gabriel's wife was from Uganda and I was surprised to see a woman of Indian descent.

'Call me Nishta,' they said.

That won't work. They'll have to get used to being addressed in other ways.

Mothers are easier: you address them by their child's name. Mai-John, if their first child is called John. But they have no children.

Gabriel must be an architect, a photographer: I'm not sure. But Nishta is a dentist. The two look identical in a funny way, like couples tend to after being together for many years.

I get lost on the way back home. This is tricky terrain for me. Harare is flat and all-sky, the roads wider. It's easier. Here, the buildings are densely packed, the streets narrow, and my vision is forced into a tunnel in the city centre, where I lose awareness of the sky. I can't navigate my way home, but the elderly ladies of the city help me out. Elderly women are the only people you can trust if you get lost, Babamukuru once told me.

Gabriel is at home when I arrive, keen to know how my day went. But my bodily cycle is disrupted, my period earlier than expected. I need a shower.

The showerhead is the size of a satellite dish, and threads of water fall on me like torrential rain. I have always liked walking in the rain. Unhurried. Uncaring. That is a freedom.

When we were driving from the airport, I learnt that Gabriel grew up in London but calls Zimbabwe home. Likely knows more than I know about the country – real things from history books, not news reports.

I'm not keen on telling Gabriel and Nishta much about my family. My father has been promised a big career move as he is one of the few Mandarin speakers in the civil service. The Chinese have arrived, and we now have a 'look to the East' policy. They want people like my father. My father is leaving his civil service job behind to be parachuted into a safe constituency as a member of parliament.

I think about my father who is perennially contemptuous of the big shots in power but loses his temper if someone is critical of the government. Only my father is allowed to take a shot at Mugabe: Mugabe is illegitimate; Mugabe is responsible for the assassination of Josiah Tongogara on the eve of independence; Tongogara should have been the leader of independent Zimbabwe. And so on and so on. But he is happy to be one of Mugabe's MPs now.

10

George prefers double-brewed coffee, and that is heresy as far as Gabriel is concerned.

'What's the point? Is it even drinkable?' Gabriel says as George pours steaming coffee into the coffee maker instead of water.

'A year from now you'll be singing my praises for expanding your provincial coffee horizons!' George grins. He's a twig of a boy, a second-year sociology undergraduate. Could be Mediterranean, Cuban, Persian, Brazilian or Cape Malay with that curly hair. He is Gabriel and Nishta's godchild; last night, he came into the house when everyone was already in bed and crashed on the sofa. I don't know why he chose the sofa and not the other spare room. It's also unclear to me why he did not sleep at his own place.

'Why on earth would you want that much caffeine in your bloodstream? A quite unnecessary buzzing overkill.'

'If it's done right, nothing beats a double-brewed coffee.'

'In my schooldays, indulging in drugs was a surefire route to expulsion.'

'I'm sorry, Gabriel, but that was back in the Ice Age.'

'You attended the wrong school, George,' Gabriel smirks.

George is still in the caterpillar costume he wore to wherever he was last night. Nishta and Gabriel told me a bit about him, but until now we've not met. I'm usually out when he's here. Once a week, he comes to clean the house for Gabriel and Nishta. They don't mind George's cleaning gig. He told them he was doing it because, he claims, they never allow him to do something for them. They came to his aid when he fell into a crisis in his first year.

'So, been up to any mischief lately, George?' Nishta bears a knowing smile. In his first year, George's course mates overheard one lecturer's wife saying lecturers who sleep with students are not adequately looked after at home. George's course mates dared him to make the woman regret her words. A week later, George had had the woman's husband on the beach under cover of night and walked into his student flat barefoot, cackling, shoes in one hand and in another a wallet, with ID and bankcards, which he had nicked from the man: proof of life.

Then he found out there's a limit to the transgressions that people will tolerate. The friends who had dared him quickly disowned him. The whole campus turned on him, pushing him into a personal crisis. But I don't see anything fragile about him. My eye is my most reliable instrument. That, after all, is why I'm at art school.

'Why not just double the coffee?' Gabriel won't let it go.

'Of course, why didn't George think of that?' Nishta rolls eyes and looks at Gabriel with bright-eyed affection as George kisses Gabriel's little bald patch and slides into a chair. Gabriel looks defeated.

A week later, he knocks on my door saying he wants to clean my room. I hope I'm not paranoid; has he changed his cleaning day?

'But you're not really cleaning anything,' I tell him.

'What do you think I'm doing?'

'I don't know.' He must know that what he is doing is not cleaning. It must have a name; I don't know it, but cleaning it is not.

'The room is not going to tidy itself, is it?' He smiles, a prankster's smile. I shut the door.

When I leave my room an hour later, I find him reading Federico García Lorca on the sofa. He lifts his head up at me, flashes a low-wattage smile and flips an inner switch that throws him back into his entranced state of contemplation. He stares into blank space as if I'm not there. It creates a finger of ice inside me.

About him, my mind is made up. So, of course, when he invites me to come along to an open mic evening in the city, I say yes. Then I poison myself with self-loathing: I can't look after myself; I must be an idiot.

The open mic venue is a small pub popular with students who look like George's kind of gang. But I find him sitting alone at a table in the corner of the room, scribbling. I never thought he was a loner. That kind of makes sense.

'You look rather dashing in this light,' he says, a delinquent glint in the eye.

'Can I buy you a drink?'

'I've no doubt you can do it. But would you like to?'

'No!' I sit down. I'm happy not to have a drink. He enjoys tormenting me.

'Okay, you win,' he grins, giving up. It's his turn to buy me a drink.

'I'll have Coke, thank you.'

'Just Coke?'

'Yes.'

He comes back with two pornstar martinis. 'They've run out of Coke, and I saw this and thought, why not?'

Everything feels like a performance.

Nishta said George's parents sold their house and abandoned London when George was ten. They chose a happier life in the Outer Hebrides. They now have a tweed business on one of the islands. George did not take the move well and started getting expelled from school.

His mother is a Zimbabwean white woman, and his father is Senegalese. But that's useless information for my purposes.

Back in Zimbabwe, his mother's parents have hired an ex-Executive Outcomes mercenary to help them turn their farm into a fortress to repel the invaders. They will be killed. I don't know what he thinks about things like that. I'm the daughter of someone in Zimbabwe's ruling party, which is hostile to white people. I should not be playing with people like George.

'I like the martini, after all. I like granadilla.'

'You like what?'

'The granadilla flavour.'

He calls it passion fruit; we figure it out. We call things different names. We're fated to misunderstand each other.

Not everyone here is a student. There's a songwriter who earns his living from busking. I've already seen a quirky vegan poet, a stand-up radicalised by the stress of making a living from running a pet lizard social media account.

George has not told me he will be reciting a poem, and I only get to know when his name is called by the MC. He picks his way through the tables and chairs. All eyes are on him. I remember Jimson having the same effect when he strode in on people playing table-football. I feel anxious for George.

He reads a poem about a boy looking for lesbian love because it is the only kind of relationship that will unlock his trapped energy. The poem is so unlike him; it's rather coy but also adds a whole new layer of meaning to our interactions so far.

He returns to his seat amid applause. I offer to buy him another pornstar martini.

In the morning, I tell Nishta that I do not want George cleaning my room any more.

11

At the end of an introductory studio practice workshop, my course mates talked about clubbing on Friday.

I knew they were going to try to make me dance and I was not ready for that. If you make someone dance, you can see everything there is to know about them.

On Friday afternoon, I left before any of my classmates could talk me into coming out.

I followed a route that took me down to the seafront. I was drawn to this vast body of water that goes beyond the horizon and up to the moon. The air temperature dropped, and a dry-cold sea breeze was cutting my exposed nasal cavity like a razor blade. A cloud of birds was shifting over the city, whipping back and forth. Every time it changed direction, it proliferated delightful shapes inside me. My interior was taking on the shifting form of the spectacle. I had seen starlings before but not such a murmuration.

At an overseas students' tea gathering someone said that if you find your mind turning inward then you've completed the first stage of culture shock: the honeymoon phase. But I was never certain about what I was going through. The frustration phase could come and go unrecognised.

I arrived at the front door at the same time as Gabriel and Nishta, who had gone out for a walk dressed like a pair of tropical birds: all bright plumage.

A couple of weeks later, while we are clearing up the back garden in preparation for winter, Harold, an old pensioner neighbour, comes over to the fence to say hello. He is wobbly old and lost his wife two years back. I have never seen him before but have heard his telephone conversations; he always yells and can be heard from the end of the road if his kitchen window is open.

Nishta and Gabriel suspect the old man of carrying a bag of disgruntlement inside him. He is friendly but also unhappy that the world is changing too fast. The country is going down the pan now that there are too many new arrivals from hot climates.

'I can see where he's coming from.' I try to make light of it later over supper. 'If white people are being attacked by the sons of the soil back home, it would be weird to not expect hostility if I rock up on these isles bearing my Bantu arse.'

Nishta and Gabriel think I mean what I am saying, I can tell. Saying 'I'm joking' will not help me. They're wearing quizzical faces now. I do not like playing at being myself because I always do it poorly; I'm always prone to doubt myself whenever I am disbelieved.

My first experience of this crippling self-doubt was at my half-brother's birthday party. Kids from the neighbourhood had come around to our house and caused mayhem. Then my stepmother discovered that the loose change she kept in a wooden bowl on top of the fridge had vanished. Her mood shifted violently. I wanted to make the unpleasantness go away. I was sure that if the vanished money reappeared, she would loosen up the air, and we could all breathe easy again.

My stepmother caught me depositing my pocket money into the empty wooden bowl. I did not even attempt to explain. It was simpler to take the bullet and say I was the one who stole the money. Even then, I was unable to spit out the self-incriminating words. A stutter came over me, fitfully, progressively, until it had claimed the entire length of my throat and immobilised my being.

Nishta and Gabriel are nice. I do not want to ruin things. I must clear the weirdness that has appeared between us. So I agree they are right; I was not joking. I loathe myself for this, after which I resent them for pushing me into a ridiculous concession.

For the rest of the week, Gabriel is busy guiding me through the twenty-first-century maze of ideas about the world, and talks about the risk, for an uninitiated African, of unwittingly taking far-right positions.

12

George's parents informed Gabriel and Nishta that they were passing through London on their way to Scotland.

I agreed when Nishta asked if I wanted to come along to meet them in Covent Garden. It was going to be my first time in London. Oddly, George had chosen not to join us.

We caught a train from Brighton to London Victoria, and I watched other trains whistle past in the opposite direction throughout the journey. What would happen if one of these fast trains went off track and came flying at us? At least back home where there was only one railway track between cities; the only danger was a head-on collision, which seemed preferable.

East Croydon station. 'Are we in London?'

'Yes. We're only twenty minutes from Victoria,' said Nishta.

Rows of gardens and houses squatted on either side of the train as it glided further into the city. Houses with rears pointed at every passenger who sails past. London was a rude city.

We caught the tube from Victoria, got out at Covent Garden, and weaved through the peak-hour crowds. The plan was to go to an African writers' event at the Africa Centre, just around the corner from Covent Garden underground station, and then to a restaurant for a meal.

When we finally locate George's parents in the hall at the Africa Centre, I find Abdul's eyes are full of life despite having prostate cancer that has put them in a wheelchair. There have been concerns that their health means they may have to leave the Western Isles.

Leah's face is alive with the birdlike intelligence I've seen on George's face. They greet me in Shona, but I do not understand them at first because I left my Shona ear in Harare.

'You've already forgotten your Shona, clearly,' they say. I'm embarrassed.

We're inside the hall at the Africa Centre. We've taken our seats, and the director steps forward. He will chair the event and invite the five writers to join him on the stage. I like this; I have never been to anything like it.

We listen to the readings and the chair in conversation with the writers. I raise my hand when the chair announces that the session is now open to the floor.

Someone invokes the popular notion of Africans writing back to Europe. Now there is no way the writers can escape pretending that what they are doing is not writing back. The audience, too, now believes it is talking back to Europe. It's such a Jimson evening.

The director ignores my hand, picking men, or women with big breasts. I watch a young man stand up; he has no question. He just wants to share his experience of oppression from inside a fancy jacket. He says he recently presented a paper on Picasso at a conference. It was received with polite silence by white colleagues. As if he had tried to talk about something that was way beyond him. Unlike him, white colleagues who wrote about African art were applauded to the rafters.

It's not clear to me if he wants to be praised like the white people or if there's another point he's making.

Gabriel gives Nishta the side look as if they are bracing themselves for me saying something gauche. Since that evening when we saw old Harold, the neighbour, I'm not sure Gabriel trusts me not to say something inappropriate.

When the chair gives me the floor, I forget what I wanted to ask. My thoughts riot, my hand stays up in the air while I try to organise my head. Either I say something crazy and face the consequences, or I put my hand down and slump into my seat, defeated.

'Africa is so rich, culturally. Hugely rich. I have never understood why Africans reach for white people's garments. And then they get upset when told the robes don't hang quite right.'

A whole bar of silence passes. Then all hell breaks loose. I'm being booed now. But I also hear rippling laughter that's clearly not directed at me. I have a supporter; I don't feel scared now. In fact, I feel alive. It is as if I have plugged into heightened awareness and know there is nothing anyone can do to me.

I can see the individuals baying for my head all around me. I see their vulnerabilities quite clearly. With a good slingshot, I could pick them off one by one. Just stand there like Jimson and go ri-ki-ta ri-ki-ta ri-ki-ta!

I am tempted to say that if things continue down that path, a cavalry of redcoats would be entirely within its rights if it stormed the building. But I have to bite my tongue.

The chair has no venom in him and will never be able to kill a person with a stare. Babamukuru Jimson would do a better job. Chances of restoring order are remote until a bear of a man in the front row stands up. He must be important because the room goes quiet. He is an old homeboy, made of sweet potatoes, groundnuts and black-eyed peas. His manner makes me feel at home again.

Then he says, 'Everyone is entitled to their opinion, which must be respected.'

'No one is entitled to an opinion! You earn your opinion by reasoning it through!' I have to shoot back before he gets a second shot in. I don't care. They insulted me.

'But I'm on your side!' he cries. He throws his arms up in the air. The chair thinks he has to step in now to regain control.

'Regrettably, we must draw this fascinating evening to a close,' he says. There's a sting in his voice now. Maybe he's a professor. Have I publicly humiliated myself?

His closing remarks include an announcement about the post-event dinner at the restaurant in the basement. We do not hear the rest because we are already negotiating our way out of the hall like an enemy convoy briefly accorded free passage during a ceasefire.

I have taken charge, but I don't know how, and I find myself pushing Abdul's wheelchair; there's security in doing something that is needed.

'You were trying to get us killed, were you?' Abdul says when we're finally at a safe distance.

'You were not going to fight for me?' I answer.

They all laugh. I'm relieved. I'd normally not talk like that to someone's dad. Adrenaline makes me bold and carefree.

13

I was unsure what to think the first time I saw George in a dress. I also feared George had venom stocked up for me underneath the dirndl.

I sought refuge in my room, where I could sit at my desk and try to do some work.

But George has plugged in the vacuum cleaner. Is taking ages to clean the floor right outside my door. It feels intentional.

Eventually, George gives up and goes upstairs. I sit in my room, thinking how mad and beautiful George looks.

When George finds me in the kitchen later, I expect provocation. George gives the mop handle a blow job in front of my face, starts performing sex with the vacuum cleaner hose and writhing on the floor with camp abandon. I will not be baited.

George grabs a chair and spins it around to sit across the table facing me, arms on its backrest.

'So why don't you want me to clean your room?'

'I'm able to do it myself.'

'Are you afraid of me?'

'I know scary people. You couldn't scare a fly,' I laugh.

'Good. We can be good sisters now.'

'Sisters?'

'Ooh, now you don't know me, sister?'

'My sister! You?'

'Ouch! So you are afraid of me, aren't you?'

'Why would I be?'

'That's a question for you to answer, dear sister.'

I was not expecting to hear my father in George, but there it is. It's not the words, because George and my father's turn of phrase could not be more different. It's not the accent; they sit on opposite ends. It's the pleasure in provocation and wielding this kind of power over the other: to corner and crush.

Less than half an hour later, I'm pacing along the esplanade. Soon, I'm way out of the city to the furthest end of the beach, where I am all alone.

My hands still tremble as if I've survived a car crash. I've relived the hour my father tried or pretended to want to kill us all. He and my stepmother had been fighting because she said he was failing to make the most of the car perk provided by the ministry. He had allowed a Toyota Land Cruiser to be foisted on him. My stepmother could not bear the military look of the vehicle. Throughout the journey, she complained about the beef at the back. We would arrive smelling like meatpackers, stuck in a car without separate air-sealed boot space as we were.

'Other men do not subject their families to this,' my stepmother said.

The sun had gone down, and we had just entered the city of Gweru. My stepmother said, 'Mugabe and his gang have long abandoned the Mao Tse-tung safari suits, wear designer and plunder the country. But they have somehow convinced you to be happy in these military vehicles that make you look like you are off to chase Renamo bandits across the Chimoio grasslands.'

After taking a lot of these little provocations, my father finally snaps. 'Now I'm going to kill all of you!'

The vehicle leaps forward as he floors the accelerator. He steers the car off the road and races straight at . . . What was it? It is dark; I cannot quite see, but I'm sure we will smash straight into a gigantic tree.

The next thing I remember is my stepmother trying to open the door. The vehicle tore through a cluster of tall prickly pear plants, and the engine stalled. My eyes are wide open, my body paralysed in the backseat. This specific sensation is the last thing I expect to return to me now. Yet I don't even realise I've abruptly stopped in the middle of the path until someone bumps into me from behind. I'm alive, shaken and shaking in Brighton.

14

I felt at home in the sculpture module and had learnt in the workshop that I needed to be controlled and deliberate.

We worked with wood, stone and metal, and I enjoyed carving. My tutor said I needed control over my technique. I tended to rush things. If you crave the satisfaction of completion too keenly, you lose control of your impulses, apparently.

We were not expected to produce anything but to get grounded in the basics of subtractive techniques like carving: removing material from a block until something, either by calculation or surprise, emerges. Not imposing form but anticipating. Not fearing mistakes because there were none.

If I could let the finger guide the chisel to respect the grain of the wood, I would be fine. Squash impulses, carve my block of wood with intention, attention and anticipation to pave the way for spontaneity, which I was told was the signature of life.

I jumped into the car behind Gabriel and Nishta on Sunday afternoon and we drove off to the bishop's evening gathering.

Every winter, the bishop activated his Church Without Walls project – a series of events for overseas students and asylum seekers.

Before fleeing Zimbabwe, the bishop was chair of the Catholic Commission for Justice and Peace's election monitoring team. Their team produced a post-election report that the government called 'provocative and reactionary'. Soon after, the bishop started receiving phone calls from the Registrar-General's office.

Then the calls started coming from the Central Intelligence Organisation. Recognising the talk of someone holding a big sjambok behind his back, the bishop did not wait to find out where this would end. The state press had already started speculating about sodomy charges being brought.

We're met at the bishop's door by Portia, a quiet and pious Zimbabwean. She's a humble, unlikely to fight off anyone or anything and leaves every outcome to God's will.

From the coats in the hallway, I'm sure I recognise George's coat, though it's possible it could be someone else's.

Two students, James and Jenny, are busy in the kitchen chopping vegetables on the table. There is no sign of George. The bishop is in the bathroom, Portia tells us. The students introduce themselves. They're South Korean; this is their second year. They enjoy busking in The Lanes on Saturdays and performing hymns. They've brought their keyboards along.

The bishop waddles into the room, bearing the bald head of the clever ant. They're old enough to be my grandfather, and must have had at least seventy rides around the sun on our planet, but they're not the calcified Christian conservative I worried about. They're in good humour, cracking jokes about how Gabriel and Nishta did well by finally bringing me along. I am quite a catch for the Church Without Walls, they say.

The bishop makes tea and coffee for us and won't let anyone help them. 'People usually do not allow me the pleasure of serving them,' they declare.

George walks in to ask the bishop for firelighters. There is another gang in the back garden trying to start a barbecue. I look the other way, regretting that I came here.

Thankfully, Portia leads George out of the room to help him find the firelighters.

I don't want the bishop to know my father is with the government, but they react as if they heard my thoughts. They smile at me and say, 'So, Shamiso, where are you from?'

A couple of beats pass before I answer, 'Zimbabwe.'

'I know. But Zimbabwe is big – have you forgotten?'

'Harare.'

'All my life, I've never met anyone from Harare,' the bishop laughs. 'No one comes from the city.'

I've given away too much info already. If I'm not careful, I will lose control and get talked into revealing my rural roots, totem and the like. People of the bishop's generation may be clueless about smartphone use, but give them your totem and one clue, and they will nail your arse down to a particular blade of grass on some dusty patch of earth in Zimbabwe.

'I'm an African,' I say.

'That's wonderful,' they remark without missing a beat.

I am saved by the arrival of my classmates Faribah, Roya and Atilio. We have little in common but fell into an alliance because we are the students whose names could not be found on a giftshop keyring at the SU shop. Once a week we leave campus at the end of the day to gather at a little place that Faribah discovered; she swears by their fluffernutter parfaits. I wish Atilio did not come along but I am learning to like him. Initially, I found him annoying and juvenile. He's not creepy though, not worth holding any hard feelings against. He came to my notice one afternoon during a lecture, when he saw that I had tuned out. He threw a paper ball and struck my nose with impressive precision. His eyes lit up, and he punched the air. Maybe because he's not like other boys and is a make-up artist, Roya and Faribah don't mind him joining our weekly café outing.

Atilio throws his arm around my shoulder as I herd them out of the room to escape the bishop and seek refuge in the back garden.

We stand outside the lounge doorway looking at the barbecue lot. After successfully lighting the brazier, George and others are having a quiet fireside chat. They turn their heads to look at us.

Moments ago Atilio had his arm on me as if he'd found a new best friend for life. He and George must have caught each other's eyes because now I sense the weight of Atilio's arm leaving my shoulder and catch him staring across the garden. And that is it: just the one look, and Atilio steps forward, at first unsure, then with intention, when George turns around and gestures with bubblegum nonchalance, arms extravagantly spread out. Meeting, they start eating each other's faces.

'Do they know each other?' Roya's eyes are popping out.

'I think it's called the flash snog,' Faribah says brightly. 'Heard it blew up on campus last year when flash mobs were all over. It's all about love on the fly. No chat involved, just eye contact.'

'Between strangers?' Roya grimaces.

'It would be pointless if you knew each other.'

Atilio rejoins us after the bishop rings a spoon against a glass, demanding everyone's attention. He sidles up to me to start a whispered conversation. He is incapable of shame. It's impossible to listen to the bishop's speech with Atilio trying to engage me. I put my defences up and stop responding altogether.

Now he starts making funny faces. When his finger brushes my neck – he claims there is a piece of fluff on my hair – I flinch but manage to throttle the compulsion to break into a run.

I shouldn't care about Atilio's choices but can't help myself. I feel betrayed. And I can't convince myself their kissing was not George making a point: that he can take anything or anyone from me. I try to see it in other ways, but I can't. I don't want to be known as the crazy girl.

I can't stay here. I need fresh air.

Soon I'm in The Lanes' cobbled streets; from there, it's a short walk to the seaside. The moon is out. Water washes up the beach, and wavelets are breaking on pebbles. I touch the water with a finger, and the sea bridles and rolls back, fizzing.

I sweep the rainwater off a bench with my palm and sit with my back to the city, trying to come to terms with what it means to have something you don't need taken away from you by someone who doesn't want it.

15

By Christmas, George had dropped his weekly cleaning routine because of his workload and I had resolved to erase him from my mind.

Nishta and Gabriel gave me a 17-kilogram piece of verdite rock from Zimbabwe for Christmas. Gabriel said it had been lying neglected in an out-of-town sculpture park that closed down.

I'd never worked on stone except for a brief encounter in the sculpture module, and that had warned me to be wary of stone. Even Babamukuru Jimson had restricted me to wood because he thought I'd be discouraged if he moved me to stone too quickly.

The 24-centimetre-long piece of stone lay on the carpet in the lounge, as if demanding to be turned into something.

'It's a special stone, found only in Zimbabwe and South Africa,' Gabriel beamed.

'I don't know what I will do with this.'

'There's no need for any action on your part. Just murmur to it on occasion, and maybe by the time you graduate you'll have charmed it into becoming something. Could be the other way around too!'

I gave Gabriel a CD, Oliver Mtukudzi's *Tuku Music*, and Nishta a book, Toni Morrison's *Beloved*.

'You have impeccable taste, Shamiso,' Gabriel said, pulling the CD out of the wrapping, trying to break it to me gently that they already own a copy.

'What quirks of fate!' Nishta was flicking through the book. 'Sorry, Shamiso, I can't pretend I haven't read it before.'

Both laughed. It had not occurred to me at all that they may already own these things. I thought I could share this with them from my life. England is a foreign place, and I do not share the same cultural references with my classmates or anyone. I have to share things to create a connection with people, though that's not always possible.

Gabriel said having two copies of the same album was great because it meant one could be kept in the studio, the long shed-type thing shaped like a polytunnel in the corner of the garden.

We had Christmas curry and went out for a walk along the beach. Several people had the same idea. We struggled to walk against a wind intent on blowing us off course with every step. I could not hear anything; all along the beach the wind was blowing every word up into the skies, and conversation required considerable labour.

I was relieved when we got back home, where we watched *Casablanca*, wrapped up in warm clothes and blankets because although the house was beautifully decorated, it was old and the insulation bad.

At the end of the evening I carried my verdite rock to my room.

I could not stop thinking about Sam in *Casablanca*. He could have escaped but chose to stay behind to entertain refugees. What a funny person. I'd rather be more like George.

16

Snow came unexpectedly after Nishta and Gabriel left for a short break. I had the whole house to myself.

I didn't want to sleep; I just wanted to watch the snow. Sometimes in the evenings, I would drag the armchair to the bay window from where I could see way down my street. I liked this kind of nighttime. I waited for the snow under candlelight; when it came, it fell steady and soft, imposing lush silence on the street.

The road was quiet; no car had driven through in an hour, and a boy and a girl had started larking about, using bicycle tyre tracks to draw figures on the snow. Eventually, they got bored, and the girl started trying to execute the surplace trick.

It was clearly a fixed-gear bicycle; pedalling backwards made it stop abruptly, throwing the girl off the bike. She did not give up but was more likely to mangle the bicycle's mechanism at this rate.

She was trying to soft-pedal, but even that was not good enough: the softest attempt at reverse cycling abruptly arrested her motion, and she would fall off the bike while the boy's face became increasingly skewed by a smirk of grotesque bemusement.

She bit her lower lip, tightening every bit of her being to direct her effort. Then a fit of frustration or something came over the girl and she threw the bike hard against the tarmac.

She picked up the bike again to give it one more try but then decided to spin around in a tight circle instead.

Then she saw me and stopped. Pointed at me. Maybe it is gauche to watch neighbours' children playing on the streets?

This is when I receive a text message from my father. He says he is in London and wants to meet. His arrival unsettles me.

The following evening I join Faribah, Roya and others because I need company and we go out clubbing.

I need the right spirit for the night, but I'm not sure how much. I crave strong spirits to deconstruct me a bit so I can put myself together again, hopefully differently and beneficially.

At the bar the cocktails are stunning, with vibrant life-affirming colours. And soon the path to discovering pleasure in throwing an arm over strangers' shoulders is wonderfully lubricated.

I love life and make lovely flash friendships, even though I cannot hold a thought in my head for more than five seconds.

When you lose track of time but feel the floor still holding firm, then you are alright. But the floor soon starts to fly away from your feet. And you are left floating in the air for a beat or two.

The hours, days and years plunge into each other until the past seems an infinite puddle. I'm utterly, merrily re-arranged.

The following morning, I wake up without a hangover. My father has already sent two messages. I forgot to reply to his message yesterday.

He is here as part of an entourage accompanying the Zimbabwean netball team to a World Cup tournament in London. I am accustomed to him allowing himself to be used by big fish even though he disagrees with them, but I'm not prepared for this: him touring with the netball team. The thought that he cares about netball cracks me up.

Online are pictures of the whole entourage arriving at the airport. There is the team at the centre of the main photograph, surrounded by an entire multitude, none of whom could ever have been to a netball match in their life.

The cabinet ministers always stand out in the crowd: two have travelled with the team. Their great fleshy folds are evident under expensive suits with buttons that could ping away in all directions at any second. Images that make you want to disown your Africanness. These comrades, I don't want to have anything to do with them.

I remember an anecdote that did the rounds in Harare a few years back. An unfortunate policeman unwittingly stops a ministerial chauffeur at a roadblock. Looking inside, he spots what looks like an epic rhino lying languid and heavy-eyed in the backseat. He arrests the driver for wildlife poaching. Then he goes about noisily demanding an obscene bribe and disturbs the rhino out of his slumbers. When the creature clambers out of the car, the officer finds himself staring straight into the deep-set eyes of the Minister of Home Affairs.

Now there, at Heathrow airport, two great rhinos and lesser creatures. That look of indecent happiness about them.

My father follows up with another text message in the afternoon: *Are you getting my messages?*

I stare at the phone, and it starts vibrating in my hand. Before I have organised my head, the call has gone to voicemail.

My father speaks softly. I cannot tell if this is in anger or something else. Underneath the softly spoken message that he leaves, I sense desperation, if not fear. He says he's proud of me. I need to laugh hard to dispel the growing anxiety and dissonance that this message produces.

17

I travel to London to meet my father. He is unknowable, despising and rejecting vulnerability with force. I'm a contemptible failure; he could not pass on to me the solid constitution he thinks I lack.

I have always been afraid of how he used to say he liked to break people and knew how to break an animal. He was proud that he intuitively knew how to locate the elusive key to an animal's transformation: somewhere in the head. He'd grab the thing gently but firmly and, at the right moment, snap his wrist in a twist that rearranged the order of the animal's head totally. And out into the world, a new compliant creature would walk.

My father's totem is the sauntering alpha baboon, Mukanya. Vamazvikongonyadza kufamba hukanyaira, vakatangi kuona zuva vari mawere; he's supposed to be the languid cliff dweller who saw the sun rising way before anyone else. His people praise the swaggering white-haired one who chose life on the rocks over tilling the land.

We arrange to meet at Victoria station. He's waiting outside WH Smith when I arrive. I can spot him from a mile. He's looking around. I don't know what to feel about him. I want to believe his message. The affection. 'I'm proud of you': it sounds so unlike him.

I sit on a bench near the ticket office and pull my hoodie over my head. He waits and waits. I watch. It is the first time I have ever had him as the object of my gaze. At art school, I've been learning how to look. You're supposed to slow down. Take your time. Observe the details. The things that stand out. And question what you see.

If I ever become a mother, I will tell my child I love them unconditionally. My love will assure them of an unconditional haven. Then, they will be free to go out into the world and question everything. Open up everything. Reinvent everything that can possibly be reinvented.

Our course leader encouraged us to attend a conference about Wilhelm Reich. Maybe it's true that sexual repression can make you a controlling person. A dictator. Repression is always the armour against feeling, anxiety and sexual arousal. I have never thought about my father this way, and if I told him, he'd return home to tell everyone that I'd lost my mind in England! A complete dunyazi!

He stands outside WH Smith. Takes a few steps forward and back. Displaying the restless dynamic of a man who has not had an orgasm in a long time, not discharged curdled pent-up energies and is looking for a quarrel.

I don't trust this.

An hour passes. How long is he going to wait? I'm beginning to feel comfortable here. There's something soothing about the white noise of the space. Every minute, there's an announcement about a train about to depart. There's a lot of people.

My father looks cross, or maybe worried, because my phone is off now.

A tannoy announcement. The voice says it's a security alert. We all have to evacuate the station. Police officers have started herding people out.

My father, I watch him walk away, one hand in his pocket, maybe jiggling coins as usual. Mukanya, the sauntering, languid cliff dweller who is always the first to see the sun rising. Travel well, white-haired one who chose life on the rocks over tilling the land. We might think more kindly of you tomorrow if we get to walk towards the sun and let the shadows fall behind us.

18

A month after watching my father in London, spring breaks out in a rash of yellow daffodils in Brighton, and I run into George with a look I have not seen before: someone has dropped all pretence and artifice as if the illusion of being typical became too expensive to maintain, and aligning outer and inner appearances became urgent.

'Hi!' I say.

They are in a flowing sky-blue silk blouse, braces and high-waisted tailored trousers. Part boy, part girl. A fish-headed snake.

Perhaps Abdul's death sparked a clarity of mind and sped up the journey towards a destination long hungered for. Perhaps it's just a coping mechanism. I don't know. A beautiful fish-headed snake nonetheless.

'I'm sorry about your dad.'

That's enough to start the tears. I did not intend to trigger them or to see this face disfigured with grief.

But George tries to regain composure and quickly pulls it together. However, their efforts are not fairly rewarded by the cosmos: a glob of snot immediately threatens to break free from their nose and stretch towards the earth. The wind blows it across their face in a flash.

Maybe this is not the snake spirit, I say to myself and laugh out loud. I half-expect George to ask what is funny, but instead it's both of us laughing now.

We meet a week later, after which I'm ready to believe that the universe does corrective accounting.

We walk to the seafront, and maybe because for the first time I'm needed, I'm not trying to fill up every silent space that appears, as I often do when anxious. I feel called to duty and willing to be George's Nyami Nyami, if that is possible. To help George across worlds. I always forget how complete and balanced I feel when I have to do something for someone who needs it.

We argue without heat over whether a cockerel says cock-a-doodle-doo or kokorikokú.

We end up larking about on the beach. And George is running backwards and playfully throwing fistfuls of wet sand at me. Missing every time. I watch George do cartwheels alone on the sand.

19

I give them iridescent scales, a glittering head, swirling motion and a pulsing stillness that lights up the room with their life force. They are the River God, the heartbeat that enslaved Africans must have sought in amulets and talismans clutched close to the chest through the length of the Middle Passage.

This is my first complete creation since I started my course. Had I given myself time to think, I'd have frozen. I had never tried anything like that before except for a figure-painting workshop where we had to produce a study of a life model over a two-day pose.

I was moving out of Gabriel and Nishta's house when George, who was not keen to go home for the summer, offered to help me move into my new room.

When they coiled into an armchair in the lounge, I knew enough to know I had to drop everything, abandon the half-unpacked bags lying on the floor in my room. I could hear the River God rumbling over the clouds in the distant horizon behind me. It was clear that they will soon fly, thundering over my head. That's when you must race to the right corner of your mind to catch them and commit them to paper before they have sailed away over the other horizon to become someone else's transition object.

After I completed the River God, two days later, I didn't know what to do with myself. I looked again at what I had produced and saw that I'd need to transpose it into a sculpture. A three-dimensional form seemed like the bare minimum for a god to thrust into life. But not on rock. Wood, maybe.

To distract myself I sang power ballads in the shower, spent hours standing under a spout that started by spitting out steam, gurgled before the water arrived and then settled into a steady downpour.

I was, of course, excited about living in a five-bed flat located above a fried chicken shop that was only accessible via a back alley with overflowing industrial bins. Universities were closed for the summer, student houses vacant and estate agents' windows were crowded with discounted rent offers.

I had chosen the largest room, had yet to fully unpack and hang posters on the walls but had vacuum-cleaned the entire flat since George left. I had never imagined this freedom, and prayed for the other rooms to remain untaken for a long time.

To keep myself occupied I decided to make fat cooks. I recalled that what made our fat cooks different was the hodzeko, which we bought from a woman who sourced it from rural areas. But you can't get that here. When I spoke to Gabriel on the phone, he said I should try kefir; with luck, it may work.

George thanked me for the fat cooks and placed the bowl on the desk in the corner of the room. Didn't bother to taste any. Maybe they were not that great; one look was enough to establish that this was bad. The fat cooks were destined for the bin.

I could not mention my enthusiasm about the possibility of making a sculpture from the portrait we made. The person I was looking at was not the same person who came to help me move into my flat. It would be embarrassing for both of us to find out they'd completely forgotten about it.

George's room was not spacious, but it was nice and surprisingly tidy. No carpet, but I liked the polished old floorboards; liked the small sofa, in the corner, recovered from a skip; liked how the theatre spotlight with metal flaps wide open was angled down at George's desk from a tall rickety stand. All this, together with the compact hi-fi set and tower of CDs by the bed spoke of an industrial aesthetic that I appreciated.

Before my next visit I considered the possibility that George was still grieving and I was in the way.

I failed to make headway talking about the books on the shelf because I didn't know how to talk about poetry.

I could have entertained George, but I'd never had that kind of talent. I would make a poor showgirl.

George's clothes, hanging on a rail at the end of the room, presented a better point of entry. I didn't think George would find it funny if I slipped into one of them for a laugh. So I asked: 'Please model the floral dress for me?'

And although I had found the courage to talk George into the dress, I met resistance. Yet it was clear that George was only waving away my suggestion in half-hearted protest. If I didn't walk over and pull that body off the bed, my chance would be lost.

George laughed, resisting gently, shyly even; I enjoyed seeing George respond to my attention in this way.

I had to take the shirt off George, who was feigning helplessness now.

'Honestly, it's like undressing a baby.'

'It's your project.'

'Good!' I said, reaching for the trousers.

'Oh no! I'm perfectly capable of dropping them on my own, thank you very much!'

'Don't worry, I won't touch your nuclear deterrent.'

Finally, the resistance was gone. George was willing to do the rest without assistance.

They pulled the dress over their head and slid it down their body while the trousers dropped to the floor, sealing the transformation.

Now transformed, George reeled the serpentine neck out of those shoulders and threw a couple of elegant shapes in brushstrokes of motion before going for the hipshot.

20

I put on George's canvas shirt and jeans, with the waistband turned down to stop them from dropping off my bum. I had not felt this way since the last time I . . . I had no recollection.

What was new was the heady rush of exhilaration that swept over me, the rebellious embrace of the fabric against my skin unlocking a new freedom.

'I'd like to own something like this,' I confessed.

'I got them from Sara's, the shop. You can borrow them if you want.'

At night I lay on my bed unable to drift off to sleep, wondering what it was that I felt whenever I was in George's clothes. I wanted to write to Farai to tell him about this.

Though I could not be certain that Farai would understand what I was talking about, he was the only person I knew who could see further than I could. He was the only one who had been able to see the possibility of transformation in Babamukuru when everyone else could only see a crotchety old man.

There was the time Farai took Babamukuru Jimson to a British Council party to see what artists look like, after he'd talked Babamukuru into trying proper Shona sculpture. At the time Babamukuru was making cigarette money from carving tourist souvenirs.

Farai had just finished his master's degree and lived with his brother next door. He had started writing art reviews for *The Herald* and *Delta Magazine* and had romantic – or cruel – ideas about Babamukuru Jimson.

Farai laid art magazines on the lawn to show Babamukuru Jimson the famous works created by the Shona sculpture movement's icons. Babamukuru examined the pieces and the wild, laconic faces of the artists for a minute and proclaimed, 'They don't know how to carve animals. That's why they make these strange, shapeless things.'

And so started their attempt at gallery art. But he was not going to abandon the animals. Things that move. They would stick to one animal to reassure Farai: his father's totem. Mukanya. Gudo. The languid cliff dweller. They came from a manless house, they told Farai. His father chose to go and work as a cook in the suburbs, kumayadi. He met his end when someone forgot to close the gate, and their big dog shot out and got Mukanya.

Farai took Babamukuru and me to the Pensão Bar & Restaurant for lunch. It was midday, too early for a band to play on the open-air stage at Pensão's garden. We found Thandi, a friend of Farai's, waiting for us. She was alone in the yard at a concrete table, reading a book.

After the meal, Farai planned to take Babamukuru to the opening of a sculpture exhibition co-sponsored by the British Council and Nehanda Gallery.

We ate, and Farai and Babamukuru did all the talking, and by the end of the meal, Thandi was bored out of her skull. She was not good at hiding it, so she dragged a case from under the table, flung it open and pulled out a gleaming saxophone. She strode over to the centre of the garden, where she struck a pose with her instrument, faced the sky and started to blow lush pathos into the melody of Big Voice Jack's 'Thata Slow'. The air was sharp with fragrant notes of jacaranda blossom. Spontaneous cheers! People waiting for the day's band started to drum their tables. I'd never seen this kind of witchcraft before.

When it was time to leave for the party, we squeezed into Thandi's truck, a battered old Mazda B3200, and set off to the gallery address in Highlands.

We got stuck at the gate because the security guard insisted that only Farai and Thandi were allowed in – the invitations could not be extended to others. The guard told us he was trained to apply the rules to strict perfection, folded his arms and put on a face of stupendous impassivity. He was unreachable now, and there was nothing we could do.

An acquaintance of Thandi, a smartly dressed white woman called Ali, a British Council representative, came to rescue us from our tormentor.

She led us into a rambling garden dotted with two-ton stone sculptures, expatriates and a rootsy squad of beer-clutching artists, musicians and poets. I was sure in that moment that Babamukuru was now way out of their depth because it was no longer clear if, by clutching my hand, they were still leading me or holding on for dear life in this unfamiliar environment. It never crossed my mind that they could be organising their thoughts in preparation for a meticulous introduction.

When we got to the middle of the garden, Babamukuru Jimson sprang to life, shaking off all my doubts and unbothered by our presence as gate-crashers. 'My name is Comrade Artist Jimson. I come from Manicaland.'

Now that heads had turned, Babamukuru switched to Shona. 'Where I come from we introduce ourselves on arrival. You don't slip into the crowd quietly like a pick-pocket.'

Farai, standing by Comrade Artist Jimson, smiled as broadly as the sun, either proud of this transformation or trying to conceal his anxiety about bringing this clodhopper who was brazenly trying to grab robes that were not theirs.

21

The bergamot scent took me back to the oranges of yester-year, to a simpler time when Babamukuru Jimson peeled fruit for us.

But it was not the bergamot I liked in George's room. It was the fish-headed spirit.

It was a happy coincidence that the scent was a portal we shared. But I didn't know how to talk about those kind of things without sounding like a silly girl who believes in superstitions. Sometimes you just keep things to yourself and note that it is an observable fact that when the scent is in the air, they come.

In the burning bush moment when my nose would twitch in George's room was when I preferred George because everything seemed simpler: they connected by subtly mirror-ing my body language until we spoke the same vernacular.

I had made some fat cooks again because, apparently, George loved them. *Those things*, they called them.

There was no scent in the air. Just regular air sweeping in through swelling curtains and out again. And George.

'One thing I got from my father.' I handed George the fat cooks.

'Your dad made these?'

'This is the only thing he can do in the kitchen. He probably wouldn't if my stepmother could do it exactly like his mother made them.'

'Do you follow a written recipe or do it straight out of your head?'

'I wrote the recipe.'

'It's not your dad's, then?'

'I reverse-engineered it.'

'What does that mean?'

'If you know what taste, what texture and so on, you can figure out the recipe by trial and error.'

'What are they called again? Fat cooks?'

'Yes.'

'Weird name. But tasty,' George said with a crooked smirk.

I wondered if George quietly resented it that I was here a lot. Here to look. I always found it hard to play cool, and sometimes came on too strong when offering my company. Now I was being denied the fish-headed spirit.

Whenever George chose to be like this, I was defeated.

George grew up trying things solo and never wanted to belong to any group. George is only now grasping the significance of drag. The magazines and books on the floor are all about drag. I knew nothing about it until George gave me a crash course last week. All these fish-headed spirits staring out of magazine pages: wild, colourful, fun, scary, bold and fearful. They tried to fit in and found out what it was like to be pulled so out of shape inside yourself that only an outburst of violence, inward or outward, restored equilibrium. At least that's what George said.

George showed me how to make a swan from a tissue, threw it into the air, and it flew around the room before dipping its nose and sailing out of the window.

'Where did you get that from?' George was mildly curious. Last week I went to see Nishta and learned that George was adopted.

'Nishta,' I say, fearful.

'I'm surrounded by people who speak out of turn. My mum, Nishta and now you. Nothing I can do about it now,' George says before speaking openly about being adopted.

We are very different, it's clear. I'd make anyone earn the right to know me that intimately. I'm a paranoid child and will not let anyone know so much that they will know which seam to attack if they want to unstitch me and pull stuff out. I envy George's courage and at once feel emotionally hog-tied in comparison.

'I guess you've never had to imagine that you might be a stolen child?'

'I have.'

'What? I thought that if you were adopted you were immune from all that. Since you get told you're adopted, you know your parents are not your biological parents, no?'

'You're dreadfully lacking in imagination, Shamiso.'

'I grew up thinking my father was pretending to be my father so that he could hold me up as an example of a good deed when he meets his creator.'

'Did your mother die?'

'Even if she was alive, someone who sells their body may not be the best person to raise a child.'

'There's a dash of colour in your family.'

Of their adoption, they say it's just a part of them that they don't want to centre in their life. And, no, they are not interested in finding out about their biological parents.

'I'd want to know everything.'

22

The first time George says it, I am unprepared.

'I love you, Shamiso!'

I take too long to answer, and there's a regretful look on their face, as if embarrassed, as if they bid too high for a cheap vase. I've missed the window.

We fall into uneasy silence. The words were beautifully delivered, but I'm unsure what they mean. And I don't trust George to know what it means to love, to commit to meeting another person's expectations and needs. Does George understand that people you claim to love feel betrayed when you fail to meet their expectations? Failure of that kind takes one through a bleak landscape of guilt and, sometimes, grief that will make you want to add to the books of the Bible. The book of Babamukuru Jimson?

But the more I think about it, the more I feel silly. Silly because I'm afraid of resetting how my head is wired, afraid to lose myself and forget all I know. Silly because it is undeniable now that when I thought I could be George's transition object, I was standing on my head.

Here I am with George, River God, flowing in and out of forms, a multitude whose variability I can only follow so far. I can't yet free myself and flow to where I'm best placed to receive and give love, but I'm alive to the bergamot scent in the room, to the George who mirrors me adorably, sensitively.

All this works wonderfully until I become awkward and doubtful. Then, this is not the thing to mirror. We must sidestep this George, who is as guileless as I am following their momentous declaration.

Now they're on the bed, and I, arms tightening around my legs, sit on the armchair with my chin on my knees. We understand each other, I think. We can't base our relationship on what we have in common. That much is clear. We can only be held together by our differences, or we'll hurt each other.

But when I return to my place that night, I can't sleep. Maybe I blew it. I should have said something. Words. Explicit words. That's how you settle things, silly, self-sabotaging Shamiso.

I listen to music on a loop while lying on my futon and staring at the ceiling, where a bright yellow mushroom grows.

In the afternoon, when I look out of my window, I see George on a bicycle, battling the dirty alleyway, rattling and wobbling uphill through flapping newspapers, rotting food and discarded takeaway boxes. Their frame is rigid and determined on a charming vintage bicycle with a basket full of goodies from a deli.

'Where did you get the bicycle?' I ask at the door.

'Borrowed it.'

George looks gorgeous in a lemon sherbet summer dress and a new pair of snazzy high heels. They are wearing perfume. They dressed up for me.

Do I also dress up, or do I play it cool?

'We're puttin' on the Ritz today and going out to look for gelato,' George says.

'Of course!' I'm open to anything. 'But what about all this nice food you brought?'

'We may need it later.'

Then George sits on my bed and helps me choose what to wear: this dress or this one?

The beach is lively but not crowded, not dense with people to the point that the air tastes like it has been breathed a dozen times over. We are not dressed to sit on the pebbles and stare out into the sea with the great unwashed.

We stroll. Arm in arm. Saying sweet nothings to each other. Watching people walking around us, people ogling us.

When George says 'I love you' this time, it feels right. There's kicking intent in the declaration.

I can't think what else to say. 'I love you' is the best sentence ever. I'm released. And I stand here with a terrific human being.

On the street, I walk with my face to the open sky. I'm in the dress and high heels I borrowed from George. The stilettos thrust my hips forward and arch my back in a lordosis posture, so my rear opens up like a glorious rosebud. I notice, now, that I am carrying a tight knot in my back, whose gnarled roots extend deep into me like a tree.

When I adjust my posture, I sense the knot loosening, and I am immediately plunged into . . . What? I have no name for this state of being.

We walk up the esplanade, two bodies inhabited by a single spirit. We walk down again. It's an ice cream day. The beach is filling up with bodies.

When our bodies lock and tense against each other, I become a body of water ready to flow in any direction, into any form or in different directions on different depths. I must take the lead, arch my body to best fit them and sync us with the graceful undulation of the River God.

I hear them rumbling on the horizon, monstrous, fearsome, beautiful, powerful and deserving only unqualified praise. George's eyes are motionless in their sockets, as one must do when trying to allow themselves to be inhabited by the River God. They stare out of pupils wild and dilated. Their eyes are fixed, bulging out of their head. I start to make animal noises and don't know if I must shut that part of me down or give in and allow myself to be carried away.

Their body coils and muscles tense as if a prayer is about to be answered; when it finally is, it's as if they have been stabbed in the chest. They gasp, recoil and collapse on me as the tail end of the spirit snake whooshes through us.

When it's over, I'm left outside my body. I can see what is in the other rooms, the neighbouring flat below and over our roof. I can see the small dog yapping its head off outside the window. I can see us from above.

23

'Let's go again!'

Again.

And again.

In the morning, when George left, I wanted to hang on to my state of perfect inner stillness. Pedestrians talking on the pavement below had taken on a languid quality. The buzzing of a bee repeatedly flying into the windowpane took on a new acoustic clarity and depth as if I had placed my ear right over the insect.

I lay there, a girl whose secret had been torn out of her and is now a perfectly free thing.

Some kind of fruit that George brought with the food shopping was still in a bowl on the table. I picked one up and examined it. Under the sunlight, its skin shone purple. At first, I did not know what to do with it. Then I cut it in half and saw celestial white segments cradled in the deep purple shell, all strangely bewitching.

At midday I arrived at my new waitressing job to start

my shift, and my first run of the day was taking an order to a customer who was sitting at the back of the café.

He was munching some fruit. And there, half-eaten in his claw, was the same fruit George had left behind.

'You don't mind?' he said sheepishly, pretending he didn't know he was not allowed to bring food into the place.

When I headed home at the end of the day, ploughing through the torrent of peak-hour pedestrian traffic, on my first turn around the block, I ran straight into a fruit stall on the pavement. There it was again: that fruit.

There was plenty of exotic fruit on display outside, but the items were unlabelled.

The following day I staggered into Sainsbury's and found right there in a heap: that fruit again. Clearly labelled this time.

After that, the mangosteen appeared everywhere: the fruit vendors at the Open Market, in The Lanes and in Kemptown, where someone had opened a little smoothie kiosk.

How had I never seen mangosteen before?

*

When I open my eyes every morning, I'm lost in delight, waking up to their face bright with animal love unqualified and total. They give themselves over to my insatiable cravings.

'There is a path for us,' George says. I don't know where this is coming from and don't understand it, but I like it.

'Whenever I don't see you for more than a few days, the patch on my breast that corresponds with the scar on your breast starts to itch,' I tell them.

Fadhili William's 'Malaika' plays on a loop all week until

it is nearly dead. George warns me to be careful not to kill songs. But sometimes I can't help it. Fadhili sings the song to console his girl when she was given away to an old man who could pay the bride price.

We spend the summer listening to music all day, flopping about on the futon with bellies full of salad. Some days we go out for a champagne picnic and come back to call the evening by way of Pink Floyd's 'Grantchester Meadows'.

Sometimes we shut ourselves in for forty-eight hours at a stretch. I listen to their every footstep on the floorboards and get to know the beat of their walk. I could pick them out of a stampeding herd of buffalo.

On some days, we don't even touch each other but are satisfied witnessing the hours come and go. I sleep like a baby, I sleep deep.

24

I should have felt altered and released when George discovered the camaraderie of the queer community but felt cheated instead.

A pretender named Sapphire wormed into George's head, and inside two weeks George went from adoring me to saying I was too much, too intense. I had seen text messages I should not have seen on George's phone, and it left me certain this was Sapphire speaking, not George.

A skinny Franco-African drag artist with spiky dreads, Sapphire spoke English that was stretched around the corners and should have been back in Africa laying retired old white women instead of causing unhappiness here.

But when George comes to my flat to fetch clothes and stuff, I beg, ask George to come out with me and meet my prospective housemates in the hope that it may postpone the inevitable. I know I can be overwhelming. I will not be intense again and will not be suffocating. I'm willing to be anything George wants, ready to disassemble and let

George put me together like a Lego toy in a tolerable shape and form. But George's mind is made up. I can't even help George pack the bag because any assistance I offer is annoying.

A little ugly moment appears when George accidentally opens the door on my toe, and I slam the door back in George's face. We're speechless; my big toe is bleeding, and I feel my heartbeat through its shattered nail.

When George leaves, I go to my course mates' new house in Kemptown. I'm scared of the emptiness of my room.

Mike answers the door and leads me through the flat and to the garden where others are chilling out on the roof. They're sitting on the ridge, drinking beer and beholding the sea in the distance. I climb up the ladder to join them on the top.

I'm about to sign a new lease to move in with Mike, Faribah, Niamh and Nick. I will be the fifth person in the house if I sign the lease and pay the deposit. It seemed like a good idea a week ago, but as soon as I'm in the company of others, I'm no longer sure about it. From the way things are set up inside me, I know that I'll find it exhausting having to be social, which is what shared accommodation demands. But I have no choice.

We sit watching our silhouettes elongate on the grass in the garden below. If I tilt my weight back enough, the centre of gravity would do the rest of the work, tip me over the edge, and I would end everything. There's no one to stop me but myself, which scares me.

'I feel dizzy. I can't stay up here,' I tell my friends.

Now everyone must go down. They're nice people; today they're in good and silly spirits. There is an argument over whether a bear does a massive poo after waking up from hibernation or how much whale vomit Faribah needs to sell to French perfumers to be a millionaire. But I'm only here in body. I'm afraid to return to my room because I know it will feel foreign, empty and lifeless.

I'm saved by Nishta, who calls to invite me to Sunday lunch. I've never been happier to hear from her.

Nishta says they miss me. They've just come back from a holiday in Malta. They have exquisite wine that needs drinking.

I take dried fruit, dates, figs and mulberries, even though they insisted I should not bring anything but myself. I hate arriving empty-handed, bearing only my mouth.

I limp all the way to their house.

'Goodness, what happened to you?' says Nishta when I arrive.

'It's nothing.'

'Anything broken?'

'No. Just the big nail.'

'Ouch. At least you didn't do it to yourself. Look what Gabriel did to himself on a boat.'

A two-foot-long fish leapt out of the water and landed on the deck. Cause for pandemonium. Pensioners running for cover. Now enter Gabriel, the hero, trying to kick the fish off the deck. His first attempt missed. Then the second one. Then he slipped and came crashing down on his side, fracturing his upper arm.

It's a nice day, perhaps one of the last splendid days of the summer. It should make my spirits soar, but I feel nothing. I'm ill-met by the formation of the celestial bodies above us and am sentenced to feel this way until the stars have found a new alignment.

Nishta orders food from a local restaurant. We carry it in trays to the table out in the garden.

Gabriel and Nishta say I can have my old room back if I want. They have had too much wine and will wake up sober tomorrow. I've spent all the summer thinking they must have been relieved to see the back of me – that finally, they were free to enjoy their house.

They're my adopted parents now. If I fell out of the sky the wrong way, they would try to catch me before I splatted on the rocks.

25

I piled my things in the boot of a cab before heading to Nishta and Gabriel's house.

I'd never been good at loading and had absentmindedly packed the boot in the wrong order: light things at the bottom. So my verdite rock, the densest item, was in a bag on top of the pile and bounced around, cracking my CDs and laptop.

I don't know why I was even bothering to take the rock when I'd felt oppressed by it since Nishta and Gabriel gave it to me. I should have abandoned it with the sketch that I made when George came to help me move into the flat. The sketch of George, of Nyami Nyami, that I no longer cared about.

I told myself I needed to get back into some rhythm in my life. Keep moving. Don't be heavy. Try to float. Soon a tide will come and help you home.

Nishta and Gabriel welcomed me with open arms. I went to bed early but could not sleep; a recurring dream about a formless thing kept chasing me out of sleep.

★

One afternoon our lecturer starts a workshop by playing a clip from the film Amistad. He wants his students to appreciate that 'often we do not know what we know about ourselves until we start telling about ourselves. Telling is an act of knowing, and that's what I want each of you to do. Tell us about yourself.'

The exercise is meant to cultivate a developing artist's sense of self and self-awareness. It should enable the student to appreciate that we each speak from a particular place inside ourselves as artists. You have to be able to conceive of your self before you can tell your story.

All I have to do is locate a place from which to speak and condense my biographical details into a narrative. Yet whenever I try to put something together, a mechanism in my head seems to malfunction. As if I headbutted the keyboard of a typewriter and the type hammers cluster-jammed mid-air, long before striking the paper.

The clip is still fresh in my memory. Theodore Joadson seeks John Quincy Adams' legal advice about the Africans at the centre of an international legal battle. Were they enslaved people or free men?

Adams: What is their story, by the way?

Joadson: Sir?

Adams: What is their story?

Joadson: Er, they are from West Africa?

Adams: No, what is their story?

Here, Joadson is lost. He is not sure what Adams means.

Adams: Mr Joadson, you're from where originally?

Joadson: Georgia, sir?

Adams: Georgia?

Joadson: Yes, sir?

Adams: Does that pretty much sum up what you are – a Georgian? Is that your story? No. You're an ex-slave who has devoted his life to the abolition of slavery and overcoming great obstacles and hardships along the way, I should imagine. That's your story. You and this young, so-called lawyer have proven you know what they are: they're Africans. Congratulations! What you don't and, as far as I can tell, haven't bothered to discover is who they are. Right?

My classmates recount their biographies like consummate raconteurs. With frightening regularity, yet another person condenses their past into an amusing nugget, complete with dramatic turns and obstacles overcome. Some speak about themselves and their families candidly. I cannot hope to match that. They are mentally lithe and agile; they seem spiritually light, if not translucent. I envy them.

When I try to write a short bio for my studio profile, I discover that knitting together a coherent story about myself is suddenly impossible. The story denarrates on its own, unravelling at the top and all the way down. As if Nyami Nyami doesn't want to be caught, not even by their tail.

Only two people to go before it's my turn. I already have the heart of a hare in blind, panicked flight.

When it is my turn, the entire room appears to swivel their heads in my direction. As if I am the star turn they have been waiting for all this time.

At first, I meet the attention with silence. Then I become terrified that maybe I will have a heart attack.

I have been here many years before . . .

When the teacher announces that some personage is expected at your school, a big man from the Ministry of Education, without prompting from anyone, you exclaim, 'The Ministry of Local Government, Rural and Urban Development is the best!'

Faces snap in your direction, and the class's collective gaze converges on you.

You're suddenly unable to speak. When the bell ringing lights up the classroom, you grab your satchel and flee, eyeballs on the ends of their stalks.

Once outside the school gate, you break into a run and race up the road in the October heat. Half a mile up the road, you stop running and kick a tin can along, hoping this might take the edge off the self-humiliation.

The tin can makes clanging noises on the tarmac. Unable to find satisfaction, you give it one almighty whack. It flies off the road to rest at the mouth of a culvert near someone's gate. A dog comes out, flying towards you, crashing into the gate. The animal follows you from the other side of the hedge, barking. Another dog in the neighbouring yard joins in. And another from the opposite side of the road. Suddenly, every dog on the street is joining in, causing a racket. You take off again.

When you arrive home, you see a white Peugeot 505 with MLG&RUD emblazoned on its front doors parked in the yard. Your father is back home early.

You burst into the kitchen, sending the two halves of the fly-screen door flying and rattling one after another. Your father and a friend from work are in the kitchen.

'What is it?' says Father.

'Hapana.'

'Nothing? Even when you look like a comrade being pursued by a chopper?'

'Hapana.'

'Hapana? What then?'

'Ha . . . hapana.'

'Nothing to what?'

'Hapana.'

Hapana. Nothing. Absolutely nothing.

You try to bolt out of the room, but your father lassoes you.

'You don't run away while I'm still talking to you. Why can't you be like other girls?'

You shrug. Now your father starts an inquisition and pokes here and there while you maintain a feral silence. The last peacekeeping soldier on Zimbabwean soil has been years gone, and your father is intent on pressing home his advantage.

Eventually, you shoot out of the kitchen in the direction of your step-siblings. As soon as you sit on the edge of the bed, your little stepsister runs to you. She buries her face in your neck, knocking you backwards onto the bed.

'Are you okay?' Nishta asks when she sees me rush into the house, slamming the door behind me.

'Yes, I'm fine,' I say. Nishta is back home earlier than I expected.

'You look like someone running away from a beheading.'

I'm about to slip out of the room when Nishta calls me back: 'There's mail for you!'

I don't want supper today. I must go straight to bed.

My sleep is shallow, but I sleep far into myself, driving far away sat next to a woman with a blinding bright lamp for a head. She says we both must find our way to the motorway quickly if we are to catch the boat before it has sailed. The car takes off like a bullet leaves a gun and the lit-up urban sprawl soon recedes in the distance, and after days in the truck we have driven far into the frosty moonlit desert that sprawls infinitely but we still blast away nightly at supersonic speed on the lee-side of the ergs and from space the truck must look like an ant taking on a cosmic vastness, and the woman splashes water on her folded hand and sticks it out of the window of the car and in an instant the water crystallises and lacquers into an ice glove, clear and gleaming under desert moonlight, before she unfolds her hand and shatters the ice glove and this spurs me to stick my head out of the window and I'm surprised by the quick and piercing sensation in the nasal cavity as I see my breath instantly freeze in the air and pelt my face but still I smile the broad smile of a clown in the rear-view mirror and laugh as we come to the realisation that though we knew earlier where we were heading we do not know any more but we know that further down the journey we must refill the tank otherwise we may have to travel at less than supersonic speed to conserve fuel and this alone will put both of us in danger of arriving after the ship has sailed away and that is why we must point the truck south-east because at the far end of the desert is an oasis on the edge of which is a sun-baked village where we arrive to the sight of wizened faces emerging from Bedouin tents, each figure stooped, eyes peering under wrinkled palms shielding the fierce sun, and soon a crowd is pressing in closely and among them observing from a distance who should it be but Babamukuru turning their turtle neck this way and that with the air of a defrocked priest and tottering towards us, but we don't have the right words yet and so flee north into the vast desert where the dunes sing and the sun scorches my face reminding me why we initially chose to avoid driving during the daytime, and in the sky two satellites orbit the earth and cloudless rain's first drop has already hit the desert, and the air is quickening with the earthy scent of rain's first contact with the parched sand dunes.

Then, at 1 a.m. a switch flicks on inside me and I sit bolt upright in my bed. I need to go for a run.

I change into my running outfit, put on my headphones, tie my shoes and bolt out of the house.

The street is dead. The neighbourhood is dead. Everyone is dreaming, talking in their sleep, and some may be even sleepwalking.

My headphones' volume is high when I set off. The music is reverberating out of my headphones and through all of me. I can see the beat with my naked eye. I run. My footsteps fall in and out of sync with the repetitive hypnotic rhythm of the music. There are moments when it feels like I'm running on Nyami Nyami's long broad back as it turns into a Möbius strip, and at other moments I feel it give way to a stoney foot-shredding broken path.

They find me unravelling, plunked on the floor of a small 24-hour supermarket with tins of dog food scattered on the floor around me. The floor is still spinning. It has slowed down significantly but it wobbles when I try to get up.

The shopkeeper and the security guard look at each other as if this is the confirmation they needed that they have a crazy girl on their hands.

'When the floor is spinning like a record player under your feet, even you would get thrown against these food shelves and bring everything crashing down onto the floor. Does that make sense?'

They don't engage with mad people, but they are willing to help them off the floor, I learn.

By the time a police car arrives and delivers me to the hospital, I am already feeling okay. In fact, I've never felt better.

26

With the beginning of the new year I wiped the slate clean and started afresh.

I had to give up meat because I intuited, from my body, that I must eliminate things that might proliferate cognitive dissonances: stuff that requires me to dissociate from the suffering of other creatures to justify my appetites. I needed a clean, translucent body before I could see myself clearly. I had never liked the stink of cooking meat, anyway.

Where I used to respond to messages instantly, I replied to nothing. If I had to communicate with anyone who resided in Brighton, it had to be face-to-face or by phone because I needed to hear my spoken voice. No email or text messages.

I needed shoes that were wide enough; if I couldn't wiggle my toes inside my shoes, I couldn't think clearly.

I had, at least, one thing to look forward to. Farai was coming to see me in March. I had not seen him in years. He wrote to tell me he was coming to reclaim the luck and fortune that I stole from him. I would be happy to let him relieve me of my kind of luck, I wrote back.

Before Farai left Harare to do his doctorate in Scotland, Babamukuru Jimson gifted him two little birds in a shoebox. The birds were not for keeping but for setting free for luck and fortune.

I thoughtlessly lifted the lid on the box, and, like arrows off a bow, the two birds shot out of Babamukuru Jimson's window into the open sky.

They flew into the pelting rain but struggled through the open air and eventually found refuge in the hedge. There, they started hopping from branch to branch, from hedge to hedge, from one property to another as I went after them, racing out of the gate, skipping over things in the drain, crouching down to peer into the hedge, and then breaking into another run. Until they vanished.

I meet Farai at the train station. I see him first and call out his name over the heads of the crowd.

He can't see me.

'Farai!' I call again. I weave through the crowd on the station concourse. When I reach him, I leap into his arms. He has to liberate himself from me.

'Chishamiso!' Farai says, holding my hand and toying with it, swinging my whole arm as if urging me to start a skipping-rope rhyme.

'That's my name! Wonder!'

'I have come to claim what you stole from me. Where are my birds?'

We laugh as if no time has passed. Like we're back in Harare.

'Chishamiso!' he repeats. As if testing that this really is me, not some ghost.

Of course it is me, I tell myself. I've never considered what made my mother give me the name. Chishamiso. But I do feel like a wonder. The hospital people said their scans revealed nothing. The psychiatry and psychology people did their tests in subsequent weeks. They also drew a blank. The psychology professor joked with his colleagues about me being a hyperreal patient. They spoke about me as if I was not in the room and for a moment sounded like my father, and that made me pity them just as I once felt sorry for my father, narrow of view and incapable of understanding I was not possessed by demons or afflicted with white people's imaginary diseases, as he claimed.

We leave the train station and pick our way down to the seafront. It's nearly springtime again, but still a cold afternoon with a blue sky. A pale distant sun hangs over Brighton, surrounded by random threads of contrails. As if a giant has been dragging a fan rake across the sky in every possible direction. I have not seen the sky this high in a long time.

I feel possessive of Brighton now that there's someone I can show around.

27

I chisel, looking for Babamukuru's face on the rock's surface.

I start with their eyes because the sooner this stone starts to witness your efforts, the better.

If a voice inside asks what to do with the unyielding rock, I tell it we must praise it. Otherwise it will humiliate you. Praise it, bargain and meet halfway, if that is what is needed.

I meet up with Farai again in London three months later, in June. I'm in high spirits because George and I have rediscovered each other.

We meet at Borough Market, and Farai comes with his Irish-American girlfriend, Emma, who has returned to the UK to take him to the US. They're an affectionate couple, and this comes as a surprise. I realise I've never seen Farai in love. I'm oddly protective of him.

Emma is visibly pregnant. She pointedly wears no make-up, and her alabaster Irish skin would burn in Zimbabwe. This might not work. I don't know. But I am happy for them.

'I'm working on a bust of Jimson!' I reveal. I've finally found a use for that verdite rock.

Farai is full of questions for which I have no answers because I don't want to jinx my progress.

'I would not be doing art if it wasn't for him,' I tell Emma. 'He tried to turn my uncle into an artist, with mixed results.'

I'm sad to see Farai leave. It's the second time he has left me stuck in a country; he's always moving elsewhere.

'I will come to America to babysit,' I laugh.

We leave the restaurant and take a riverside walk to Embankment, where we say goodbye because I can't wait to return to George.

At the end of the month we take a road trip to Italy. George, who is a year ahead of me, has graduated and is unburdened.

They are behind the wheel, and I sit beside them, floating inside. Nishta and Gabriel have lent us their VW Beetle on the condition that we buy insurance to take care of any problems that might arise.

The eastern sky is orange. It is the last full moon of summer. I still fear the sin of naivety and its long tail of corrosive self-recrimination. I carry repressed terror and crazy hope, both mind-altering substances.

We catch LeShuttle across the Channel, and on the other side, we roll out of the train, and George's eyes are wild with optimism. We tear down the autoroute, singing along to Sade's 'Smooth Operator'; they check the mirrors and slalom through the lanes like James Bond.

'You've turned into a proper hyperreal African, Shamiso, haven't you?' George says later, seeing me brush crumbs off my dashiki dress. They're determined to wind me up until I abandon my dress and leap into theirs.

I have never been on a road trip this long before. We glide through France, the autoroute becoming a silk ribbon gleaming in the distance, going up and down across valleys. We stop to eat and refuel a few times or to photograph the sky, which hangs bruised by the sirocco on the distant horizon.

Then we pursue that patch of sky. It floats in the middle of the windscreen for hours. A low-flying MiG jet rips across the motorway at a ferocious tilt, and a flock of terrified birds whoosh like arrows and fly straight into the tarmac. I pinch myself to confirm I'm not in a dream. I have seen birds fly into vertical surfaces. Birds flying into a horizontal surface is a first.

By the time the city of Dijon appears in the distance like a mirage, we have stopped talking. We have also long tired of music and just commune in silence.

After checking in at our B&B, we dump our bags and seek fresh evening air and food.

A Malian youth in a dashiki top and a sharp sculpted Afro plays the piano in the open air at Place de la Libération. Le sans-papiers is playing Chopin. A crowd has formed around him.

I put on a kente dress in the morning, and we point the car towards Lyon. Then Nice. We are rolling into Nice when the car's dashboard starts flashing temperamentally. The rescue crew find us fanning the still-smoking engine with a newspaper on the hard shoulder. The monobrowed mechanic orders a tow truck and says the car will not be ready for at least a day.

We spend the afternoon on the beach where two schoolboys approach us.

'Avez-vous des lunettes de soleil?'

George looks like they will die of laughter. 'This happens when you wear kente or dashiki,' they say and tell the boys I'm a hyperreal African and they should not expect sunglasses or watches from me. The boys walk away mystified.

Our insurance allows us to hire a car from the garage since a spare part will take a week to arrive. They give us a brand-new Audi. It looks tiny but feels magically vast once you are inside.

'It's big enough for us to start our own tribe, complete with a complicated gift exchange system,' George says.

They inform me that European tribes get a bit African the further south you travel down the continent.

'They're our brothers! They're louder, upbeat, talk with their hands and aren't too fussed about time,' George laughs.

We spend a night in Turin, and I fall off my style horse the following morning. I must abandon my dashiki and kente for a designer flannel shirt and corduroy trousers. I just need to blend in a bit to feel nicer inside. George says I am now promoting vulgar Western emporiums of consumption.

'Your struggle credentials are ruined!' they torment me. They will not stop until I'm inside their dress.

Later in the day, we are on Piazza San Carlo, dodging Vespas as we join loved-up couples walking arm in arm.

We sit and watch families promenading with their lustrous-haired children.

We wander through the old city and end up at a trattoria where we buy pizza and walk through the backstreets to sit on a bench in a secluded cobbled little square. All around us are doorsteps on which a few senior locals sit, staring out in enigmatic silence.

We eat, laugh and point at pigeons and objects with our toes. I throw a piece of pizza at a pigeon and set a whole flock of birds flapping in the air. Seconds later, we are in the thick of beating wings, hair being pulled every which way. We run, hands and arms over our heads.

Twenty-four hours later, we are driving out to a mountain village to throw coins into the village well and make wishes under the sorrowful gaze of a fresco of the Virgin Mary.

28

Something was not quite right.

After Italy, George came to my place to dress me up as Captain Thomasina Sankara: a military-style shirt with rolled sleeves, a red beret slipped under the shoulder strap, and scarlet lipstick. I was George's creation, and I still loved that, loved that we were each other's creations.

George was in Carolina Maria de Jesus attire: a slum frock and headscarf.

George wanted to go out because some of the people from the Rainbow Quorum Club on campus were going to a club in Shoreditch. Sapphire was going to be there.

'I don't know what you see in Sapphire,' I said upon hearing George's proposal. This was too sudden, with no prior warning. 'I don't like permanently feeling as if I'm about to lose you to someone, and I think sometimes you're intentionally making me feel this way. I'm not a teenager any more; if you can be honest with me about what kind of relationship you want, that would be helpful, because then I will be able to make an informed choice about my life. I won't allow myself to be pickpocketed in broad daylight again, George.'

George understood I was ready to end things, was subdued for a couple of days, but, as a compromise, agreed we should go to the Africa Centre bar. There we sat, facing each other, short of words and unsure who was the torturer and who the tortured.

A man was holding court at a table in the corner of the bar, lambasting the many Africans who had supported Mugabe as he brutalised his own people.

'Mugabe was disappointed that Bob Marley was invited to perform at the independence celebrations. He thought Rastafarians were pot-smoking layabouts, and he would have been happier with Cliff Richard!' he laughs.

He is enjoying himself, maybe spirited into life by the bottle of Zambezi beer in his hand.

When he gets up, I notice he is very tall. His stride is ghostly, like something from a Juan Rulfo story. We must have caught his eye because here he is, almost at our table. He looms over us as if he's spotted something wrong with us. Or maybe he's forgotten his pick-up lines.

'Please sit down; you're making us nervous,' George says.

He pulls out a chair and plonks himself down, saying, 'I'm Joel.'

I get a consolation look as he quickly turns his full mega-watt attention on George.

'Very long feet, I see. Hmm,' George says, and they both laugh and exchange light touches on the knee. George is enjoying the attention.

'Will I ever be enough, George?' I stab.

Of course, we must fight. We must be unkind to each other in front of everyone, and I'm not going to back down; neither is George.

Whatever little dignity we had when we entered the bar, we leave without it, afraid to acknowledge that what we did to each other there is unspeakable.

Too scared to face the ugliness we displayed in front of a full bar, once out on the cobbled stones of Covent Garden, we seek shelter in each other's arms. Hold fast and hope that this will not be the night that changes everything.

We arrive bleeding at a joint in Soho, relating to each other like porcupines in winter, needing each other's warmth but careful not to get too close to be stabbed by the other's quills.

The lounge bar is, therefore, not quite right: a cosy affair of plush velvet sofas, ambient lighting and relaxed elegance; acid jazz playing when one needs loud and violent music. We must be the youngest people in the room. On principle, I don't go to places where my fashion sense might be regarded as a hate crime, but I agreed to come here and can't change my mind. I must keep the peace.

There is still love. There's still a heartbeat. I still appreciate George gliding across the floor on the way to the toilet because George knows how to walk and no longer needs a tune turning inside the head to walk gracefully. I have no doubt this is what draws Caitlin to us when she comes to compliment us on our looks.

Caitlin wants a picture, if we don't mind, which of course we don't because we crave a little sugar in their souls, especially from someone who is clearly our superior in experience and circumstance and initially speaks to me in French because she mistakes my accent for that of a French speaker. She emits the charming confidence of someone with an education that enables them to experience the world in several languages. She would know where to buy a good vase, a good dress and where to find both Michelin-starred restaurants and hidden-gem eateries in London. An easy person to trust.

Before she leaves, she digs into her tote bag and pulls out her business card. It is fitting that she works for a modelling agency.

I would come back to this evening a thousand times over to see what I could have flipped to shunt the course of things onto a different track.

I slide the card across the table to George; it's George who Caitlin is after. It's George who has star quality. Photogenic, clever, not too black, not too white, queer and someone who knows their kombucha from their Kompany. Ticks all the boxes.

'She's got her eyes on you, not me.' George pushes the card back. It's the first sign that it's over. There's a look I've not seen before on George's face.

We argue about it, to the ridiculous point of considering calling Caitlin's number to settle the argument, but that would be the quickest way to give a terrible impression.

'We'll drop her a line tomorrow.'

'Allow a decent number of days to pass first.'

'Anyway, the card is yours, Shamiso.'

'You're not going to call her without me, are you?'

'Goodness, don't you trust me?'

'I do. Of course you can call her alone. That's fine.'

The following day we call Caitlin. We lean into the speakerphone in George's room, trying not to breathe.

The call is brief, and a long silence follows after George hangs up.

'She chose you because of where you come from,' says George casually. This is not George but a body inhabited by a malevolent spirit. I'm afraid this devil will pack me in a bag, throw me over their back and clickety-clack straight down the hill.

29

I meet Caitlin in a Caffè Nero in London and, by the end of the day, I've signed on the dotted line.

The fee for the development programme is steep, at £1,500, but I'm lucky to get away with an initial payment of £500. I can pay the balance in instalments, apparently.

I will attend three masterclasses and a photo shoot in the Maldives. Mingling with beautiful, sharp and stylish people, and attending a glamorous party hosted by Naomi Campbell, will open doors to worlds I have never imagined.

I try not to think about George. I can't stop thinking about Caitlin: her sophistication, her obliging disposition and the delicious attention she gave me.

By the end of summer, Caitlin has stopped responding to my calls and messages. And George is ghosting me. Well done, Shamiso.

I turn to books, magazines, sad music and terrible movies to learn how others before me handled setbacks. Some do so by accepting they can't change anything but themselves.

Some cry themselves to sleep and see themselves flying away or dying in their dreams. Others stare blankly at the hand they'd been dealt and no longer get drunk, no matter how much alcohol they sink into their bodies. Some fight.

I sit cross-legged and impassive, realising I lack a set of life principles with which to meet the world. I don't know what to do and only crave the trueness of things. I need to evolve fast but don't know how. I have no plan, no method, no technique or style. I've even forgotten how to walk with a tune in my head. I must start somewhere.

At the beginning of the year the Education Secretary comes to open an exhibition at the new gallery on campus.

She marks the opening by cutting a cake in the shape of a naked African woman that is intended to celebrate the spirit of artistic freedom and the artist's right to be provocative. And the crowd claps. How can they not see this? They're not horrible people. Some of them are my classmates. And faculty staff, they are usually, though not always, eager to help. But they're always kind, apologetic and painfully embarrassed when they drop the ball. How can they not see this?

'How can you all not see this dubious gesture that enables the daily structural re-traumatisation of whole communities?' I have to shout at the top of my voice.

'If the Education Secretary is here to celebrate artistic freedom and the right to be provocative, we must also be free to be the same. It cuts both ways! You cannot want freedom for yourself without wanting it for others unless you're a hypocrite.'

People are terrified when you start smashing full wine

bottles on the fancy light fitting hanging over the minister. They trigger anti-terror measures if you carry a big backpack, even if it's only full of groceries.

You stop a security bloke by smashing a full bottle in his path. Do it like you mean it, and people quickly sober up.

30

You sing from your stomach, says Lucinda, who patiently takes me through the techniques. We're meeting for the first time. I'm uncomfortable jumping straight into a class of mindful singing, so I booked a one-on-one to find my feet. Nishta's recommendation.

Lucinda walks me through the stages. I must always be aware of the changes in my bodily sensations and be able to follow them. I must be totally present.

I'm surprised by how much better I feel afterwards.

'If it feels impossible, it's because you've forgotten to keep breathing,' Lucinda guides me.

I'll have to be in the studio at odd hours when no one is there. I need to chisel and hum in privacy; I need something to stop me from thinking about the coming hearing.

One day I work twelve hours without a break.

A couple of days before the hearing, I join Lucinda's class for the first time. There are a dozen people all together, a dozen voices.

Towards the end of the class, Lucinda brings all the voices together in harmonies: the coming home part of the class. I surrender to the voices catapulting me into whatever this is that calms the tempest as evening falls quietly on this corner of England.

After the class I walk home. I feel indifferent to the outcome of my disciplinary hearing in a week. I'm ready to leave the country, leave Europe. Escape European languages, their highly gendered grammatical structures that simplify so much you can slice a black woman without seeing what you're doing. The disciplinary committee will think I'm insane, but they're thinking people; they will understand when I say Africans become homophobes when they learn to speak European languages, that they love the macho far-right Western politicians when they cease to see that we prioritised other categorisations over gender until we learnt to speak European languages. They must understand that languages produce different worlds.

On the day of the hearing I count my steps through the corridor to the room I was directed to.

They are all waiting for me when I walk in. There is no black person on the seven-member panel, but there is an Asian woman; the required boxes have been ticked.

They are all experienced people; with their minds they will be able to see me from every possible angle. They're not going to be fooled by an undergrad.

But when my course leader says I'm an 'astonishing liability', his register is over the top. He sounds bombastic and out of character. He has probably joked about this case over a bottle of claret with friends or family. Telling them how a Zimbabwean student has put them in a terrible position.

Gabriel said he had heard that my fate was unlikely to be decided by whether I had messed up or not but by departmental politics: one clique's agenda against another.

I leave the room feeling optimistic and relieved I did not need to make crazy arguments.

In the morning, I learn from a call that I've got the support of the SU. The police are apparently reluctant to press charges, in case it triggers wider student protests which they are not resourced to handle.

'You're very lucky,' says the bloke at the other end of the line. 'Now, let's keep your halo polished and out of any more mischief, eh?'

I'm overdue luck, I think. But I can't sit still while the disciplinary panel's decision hangs over my head. I have to keep moving. Walking. Humming low frequencies through the pit of my stomach. I spend the day wandering aimlessly through the city.

I strike up a conversation with a Sudanese refugee in a bus shelter. His name is Manu. He spends his days patrolling the beach and the streets, arms covered in replica watches, a winning smile and a song in his heart.

'I can help you sell your things if you want. I don't want anything. I know how to sell; I've done this with my uncle before.'

But Manu won't move. He wants to go but remains rooted to the spot, smiling at the sky like an enigma.

I leave, baffled, only to see him later running towards me as I leave the beach.

He's waving a £20 note. It's what was under his foot. This is why he could not afford to move an inch. The note fell off some youth, and Manu immediately put his big boot right over it. But the youth and his mates would not go away, certain that he dropped his money at the bus shelter. Manu held his nerve. He won.

We celebrate his win with cans of Coke from the kiosk on the beach. We don't sit but walk and talk. In the distance, a ship and a tugboat are sailing down the English Channel. By the pier, a powerboat under the control of a madman is making a continuous heel turn, creating a whirlpool.

'I want to drive that thing one day,' Manu says. He was briefly a soldier back home, but the uniform put him off. The uniforms got thrown at them from the back of a truck, and you had to catch one, or you'd have nothing. You had to make do with whatever size you got. He's tasted the humiliation of fitting into Africa's smallest pair of trousers. He will never again allow anyone or anything to ask him to wear something he did not choose.

The disciplinary panel's letter arrives a week later. It's a five-page PDF attachment, the contents of which I'm too emotionally and cognitively overloaded to process right away. At least I retain the capacity to do a document word search. Zero hits for 'expel', 'expelled' or 'expulsion'. That's all I need to know.

31

I was about to graduate and was faced with a choice: to stay or return to Harare.

I didn't want to be here and didn't want to go back to Zimbabwe. I was not going to get a visa to remain in the country since I had studied the wrong subject. I should have studied medicine.

If I had the right passport, I would have considered packing my bags and going to continental Europe. Maybe Berlin; it's the only city my coursemates dreamt about.

If I won the American Green Card, I could live in New York. If I was a refugee, I could get into Canada. Australians would throw me into a floating prison.

Or I could change how I saw myself in one stroke by remaining in the UK. But I could not find the answer to why I wanted to stay in Europe, speaking the languages while my mother tongue withered away in my head until there's little trace of it.

Gabriel came to my graduation ceremony, but Nishta could not make it. She was already ill.

I was going to stay in Brighton until the new year to give Nishta time to recover from breast cancer surgery.

Nishta and Gabriel were relieved when I moved in again.

I had noticed they could get a bit cold and impatient with each other. Sometimes cruel. A third person in the house would inhibit unkind displays.

Often Nishta and I would talk ourselves empty and sit quietly in the garden when the sky was clear. Let the wind speak.

She was anxious about her position at the dental surgery. Her partners had offered to buy her out.

At the beginning of December, I accompanied Nishta to the hospital for her last chemotherapy dose. We sat in the waiting room, going through another cancer diet recipe book and crossing out all the recipes Nishta did not like. When we'd been through the recipes, she informed me that she was considering visiting Uganda.

Nishta had not returned to Uganda since Asians were kicked out of the country. She was seven when her family arrived in the UK. The family never spoke about what happened in Uganda but sometimes reminisced over how marvellous it was and what they missed about the country.

'Why would you want to return to a place that traumatised your family?'

'One day, you too will want to visit Zimbabwe.'

Nishta spent the subsequent week recovering in bed, drinking ginger or milk thistle tea. Sometimes she'd come out of the house and sit on the bench in the garden, soaking up sunlight when it appeared. Sometimes she'd rest in her armchair in the lounge, drink tea and fall asleep.

One afternoon I also fell asleep. I dreamt that a gaggle of screaming boys was chasing me. They were ravenous for violence and cruelty. They want me. If ever there was a time to run, this was it . . .

The path is narrow and muddy. I splatter through puddles. They are gaining ground. My shoes, suddenly unlaced, threaten to fly skyward. I splay out my toes inside each shoe, and with this bit of effort, I am transformed. Fierce as a toad, I apply myself and my shirt starts to flap and snap in my wake.

Surprising myself, I come to a halt, pick a long stick and decide to stand my ground. I swing my stick once, twice and one more time, menacing and scattering the pupils with precocious ease. They look surprised, fall silent and look at each other, looking for leadership. They are a headless mob now. I could drive them back with my stick if I wanted. Not one of them has the bravery to lead.

Triumphant, I pirouette and splash through a great puddle. Now I put on a show, show them a clean pair of heels.

32

In the new year, when I was done sorting and discarding what I had to let go of, I could fit what remained into two suitcases.

On my last morning, I woke up ready to bid Brighton farewell, only to hear from Nishta and Gabriel over breakfast that George had vanished.

'I think it's my fault.'

'Nonsense!' said Nishta, rubbing my arm.

The last time I had seen George was five months ago, just before I moved back into Nishta and Gabriel's to help out. George was at SOAS London but still lived in Brighton. We had not spoken for over a year since the Caitlin episode. Then I ran into George in North Laine. George, mother and new girlfriend, Astrid.

It was still fresh in my mind, like it had happened yesterday: my eye caught them when they were barely three steps away, heading straight to me. I spun around and pretended to look at stuff in a shop window, hoping they wouldn't see me. The display was packed with vibrators and dildos in every shape and colour.

'Shamiso! Which one are you after? Let me guess!'

I was still scrambling for a reply in my head when George's mum caught me off guard with a hug and asked how I was getting on.

'Bon!' I answered.

'Bho Bho!' she smiled.

George introduced Astrid, a fairy-like thing with the kind of striking looks that often compel people to equate beauty and morality. I already knew her through George's social media feeds, knew her tastes from the curated playful front presented, and knew she had a hunting suit and ate beef. And this is where I got lost trying to follow George's choice: kissing a carnivore.

George's mother looked pleased. I felt sorry for George and was able to find it in myself to at least look happy for the couple.

I gave everyone sincere hugs when we parted.

A couple of days later, George appeared at my doorstep, moving around my flat with a familiarity that comforted and unsettled me. George does not understand that people die for this kind of carelessness. You don't pop in and out of people's lives whenever you please.

George has always liked dressing me up. But because we never resolved things explicitly, I can't allow myself to be as George expects. I know how to conceal myself: George will have to put in more effort but won't be able to reach me. I don't want to be found. I can now look at myself in the mirror and accept what I see. That's all I can do. What

I won't do is be left holding the bag, weighed down by guilt. I did not ask George to come here.

When I start to feel like I'm being rearranged inside, as if George has dipped a finger into my interior and started to stir around deliberately so that an insistent undercurrent starts to swell, I have to block here, there and again there – block every attempt to stimulate.

'Why are you doing this, George? Why now?' I pushed away George's hands.

'Because I miss you,' George said quietly. 'And because I owe you an explanation.'

'Okay.'

'I was scared, Shamiso. I was scared and embarrassed because we didn't handle things well.'

'I think we did reasonably well. Except maybe for that . . .' Our mutual reluctance to confront 'that', revealed an unsettling truth: it is far easier to appear enlightened about race when it is someone else's story.

George nodded.

'And I don't mind being a diversity and equality Barbie as long as we talk about how and why. Otherwise, conversations that should be exploratory become minefields.'

'That was awful. I shouldn't have said that. Honestly, I don't know where it came from.'

'Manthia Diawara gets tortured worst by West African immigration officers whenever he lands in Paris and presents his American passport, which shows he was born in Mali.'

'I didn't torture you, though. And it didn't help that you couldn't speak up, either.'

'I'm glad we're reconnecting pieces of the puzzle.'

'I agree.'

Then George confessed to making fat cooks for Astrid. Using my recipe.

'I'm wondering now, how much of you is real? Everything about you, how much of that is real? How much has merely been a repetition of things stolen from your past relationships? You pretend to have something unique going on, but there's nothing there, clearly. You take my recipe, my family's recipe, and use it to recreate what we had. What else do you do? Do you have sex to our music?'

Head in hands, George invites a machete to the neck in the way people do when unaware it's inevitable that the blade must now come down hard and swift.

Gabriel and Nishta drove me to the train station and we didn't mention George once. The police said they had no resources to look for every adult who might be getting shit-faced in some place, as people often do. George could be in Senegal or Zimbabwe, searching for an uncomplicated anonymous life.

I said goodbye to Nishta, Gabriel and the city at the station and caught the train to London.

I thought about England's ghost train network. It criss-crossed the country and was created by a nineteenth-century statute to maintain a legal fiction that this or that train route remained alive. Every Tuesday, a ghost train departed from Brighton, carrying no one and nothing. It went through London to Gerrards Cross in Buckinghamshire before returning to Brighton.

33

I heard the hum for the first time in London. A diesel engine idled in the distance all night. Not everyone could hear it.

My studio was on the top floor of the Old Sugar Mill, a once-derelict riverside factory building that now housed a community of traders, artisans and artists.

If I wanted to escape the hum, there was always a party where I could look for people like me, and if the night ended before I had found a body to take home to put a little sugar in me, sometimes I wandered back to bed in the small hours, empty and already hungover under a full moon.

After hopping from one London postcode to another for years I moved into a flat in Silk Square and became a cat person when a homeless Norwegian Forest Cat adopted me.

I brought Muffin into my flat later. Nishta had her delivered to me after her mother passed away. Muffin is now queen of the neighbourhood. Her GPS tracker says she can wander up to half a mile from my flat.

At first, I feared she might not get along with the Norwegian Forest dude. The Norwegian became homeless after the family who owned him sold the house and migrated to sunny Australia. He was supposed to be inherited by the house's new owners, but they brought two big dogs, and the Norwegian moved out to join the homeless ranks.

I had just become acquainted with Tony, a Trinidadian old-timer, a builder well past retirement age. They were always doing house repairs on the square. Said they work because if you stop, you start to disintegrate from the head down. Years back, someone hired them to refurbish a house on the square. While at it, a neighbour asked if they could look at his house's plumbing. Then someone wanted his roof repaired. And so on and so on. Now Tony is a permanent fixture.

We used to pass each other silently until they started repairing the house next door. Then we started talking because, in good weather, I liked sitting on the doorstep on weekends, watching the world go by.

The first time I found the Norwegian in my kitchen, I told Tony about it. They told me that the cat ate from every kitchen in the neighbourhood. Few people knew his name; he was called different names depending on whose house he was in. But he had to answer to 'Babamukuru' to earn food in my flat.

When I told Tony I had brought home a new cat, Muffin, they said I was in trouble now. 'How you going to keep the new cat inside for weeks and not shut out your old friend?'

So I kept Babamukuru and Muffin in the flat for four weeks.

The first time I let the cats out, Babamukuru shot straight off and went to the front garden wall where he liked to spread himself so every passerby could stroke him. Muffin sat on the doorstep observing.

Tony stopped by to stroke Babamukuru.

'Out of jail, I see.'

'He was not in jail. I had to keep him inside so we could get to know each other better.'

Tony asked if I knew the woman who lived in number 25.

'No.'

'She's also from Zimbabwe.'

'Really?'

'Yes. Husband is Swedish. But she's from Mutare!'

'You talk as if you know Mutare!'

'Undoubtedly, I do.'

'Really?'

'I visited in 1982. My brother is a doctor and still lives there. We don't talk much now. Family quarrel.'

Their brother was one of the Pan-Africanists who were romantic enough to decide to settle in Zimbabwe after independence.

'Bet your brother feels proper conned,' I laugh.

'We stand for something! You stand for nothing!'

'You're lucky you're not on a walking stick yet, or I'd have kicked it right out of your hand.'

'I rest my case.'

Six months later, Tony desperately knocks on my door. It's a Saturday afternoon. Babamukuru is being ripped to shreds by dogs. Two pit bulls are shaking him like a rag doll on the pavement, their tails vibrating with killer impulses. There's already a small crowd, and no one knows what to do.

'You're supposed to hoist the dogs' back legs up!' I'm screaming at the owner, who seems utterly out of his depth, kicking the dogs to no avail.

I've never done it before and have slipped into a zone where it's hard to tell stupidity and courage apart. I yank one dog's legs up, and it lets go. It wriggles powerfully, athletic and muscular, and I cannot hold it up for more than a few seconds. The instant I let go, it's back on the attack.

The owner lifts the other dog's legs and hoists its whole body up, but just like me, he cannot stop it from shooting back to Babamukuru as soon as he puts it down. My second attempt is no better. The animals are taking their turns now. A couple of neighbours step in to assist.

Then, a miracle: Tony, thank God, somehow manages to snatch Babamukuru's body and makes an almighty dash into my front door, slamming the door behind them as the dogs crash into it.

The man calls his dogs. No apology, no contrition. Nothing. He does not engage with a single person. A new kind of being, he's beyond tagging. He looks dangerous, like someone long disqualified from society. He takes his gaunt face and dogs and hurries out of the square with everyone still in a state of shock.

34

On the wall where Babamukuru spent most of their days stretched out soliciting strokes from passersby, I place a message informing people that Babamukuru is gone. There will be a gathering to give them a send-off on Wednesday evening. No speeches or the like.

I watch a heap of flowers and cards steadily materialising over days on Babamukuru's spot.

On Wednesday evening, people start trickling in, familiar faces I've never exchanged a word with. Big cities are strange that way. You can live on a street for years without ever speaking with a neighbour a few doors down the road. And it's not that they're unfriendly; they're friendly people. A dozen are already here.

A young lady in laddered tights joins us. Heroin chic, which looks very retro nowadays. A half-full bottle of peach schnapps in one hand, as if she was out of the notorious big house across the street, where they shoot porn. If I were from that house, I'd also want to torment the ordinary polite gentle folk to whom this kind of freedom is savage, dangerous, yet lusted after.

The sound lady waves a hand, 'Hi, everyone. I'm Anaïs.'

The neighbours respond with polite indifference. Initially bemused by the reception, the young lady now wears a contemptuous smile and tilts her head back when she drinks. She stares unblinkingly at the couple from the corner of the square.

The bouffant-haired lady who only walks the dog at midnight comes over to grab a drink. This one loves to drive into the heaps of leaves left by street cleaners, ready for collection. Scattering them wide. I can never tell if it's out of delinquency, joy or spite. I see this every autumn.

The lady asks why I called the cat Babamukuru in my note.

'What do you call him?' I ask. I already know that Babamukuru is Jack in the kitchen of the American dude who lives in number 18. 'Everyone seems to call him whatever they want.'

'His name is Hank!' says the lady.

'Is that what you called him?'

'That's his name. That's what everyone calls him.'

Later, the lady comes back to apologise for sounding rude earlier. It's Sylvia, a senior resident who has lived in the square for a lifetime and used to own Babamukuru's mother. Babamukuru was born nineteen years ago.

I pass Sylvia off to another neighbour, Rosie, when I run out of conversation.

'Where are you from?' Sylvia asks.

'Liverpool,' Rosie says.

'I'm from Liverpool too.'

'Where in Liverpool?'

'Maghull.'

'Ain't really Liverpool, though. We call you woollybacks,' Rosie laughs.

More neighbours are still arriving with more drinks. Even Rob steps out of the flat next door. I regret giving in to this when my body needed a little joy. Rob's tongue is quite the swordfish: I had to bite it to stop the assault. Rob is also the speedy type and rushes to the end of his prayer when yours has barely started. Once Rob says amen, you have no choice but to open your eyes.

The man who looks like a retired headteacher is a former Tube driver. He has brought his teenage daughter, who is still at school and smokes like a trooper when the parents have gone to bed. Every night from the window on the top floor of their house, I see the girl switching off the light in the room to light a fag. Quiet and sweet but suspicious. I try to tell her wordlessly that 'your secret is safe'.

'Would you like a kitten?' I ask. 'I have four left. Two months old.'

The girl looks to dad for approval.

'You selling them, or are they up for grabs?'

'It's bad luck to flog animals you didn't mean to breed, innit? I should have had my Muffin spayed but knew nothing about cats.'

The dad approves, and the girl and I leave to get the kitten.

I walk out of the flat with the girl as Tony arrives and starts setting up a portable barbecue in the front garden. I thought it was an empty gesture, all that talk about doing jerk chicken. But here we are: a massive load of chicken and a bag of charcoal.

Soon Tony is standing by the grill, turning and poking pieces of bird sizzling over the coals.

'When was the last time you were back home, Shamiso?' Tony asks casually.

35

*So you spent four years hiding in Andalusia's white villages and
returned to the Outer Hebrides to seek a quiet life.*

I started the letter after midnight when London was asleep.
When I could hear myself better. Speak to the full moon,
the only thing both of us could see in that hour if George
was still awake.

I wasn't sure what to say about myself. I was managing
to pay both my flat and studio rent bills but not without
waitressing one evening a week. I'd only had to throw a
rent party once in my studio to get me through a rough
patch. I was not in danger of joining the foodbank queues
and had learnt to be frugal. I was not at risk of eating
industrial meat though the vegan lifestyle was now beyond
me. I had an allotment plot that produced most of what I
ate. For an illegal, I was okay.

I put the letter in an envelope with a Nyami Nyami
pendant I had carved in my studio.

I heard nothing back. Winter came and went, and so did

spring. I could not tell if George was too wounded to reply or did not want to know me any more. Because I could not bear the silence, I travelled to Scotland in the summer.

I caught the sleeper to Inverness.

The train motion was comforting, but I could not sleep. The patch on my breast that corresponds to the old scar on George was throbbing. I remembered George talking about the scar, a consequence of falling on a barbed wire fence when George was at school. Sometimes, it was as if it had started to move across my chest. I squashed it.

In the morning, I woke up and ordered coffee at the buffet car, where I shared a table with a retired vicar who said I looked like a woman from the Douglas clan. I couldn't tell if he was being nice or horrible, but he said their motto is 'Never Behind'. Only then did it become clear this was the tongue of a good-natured barn owl.

'Coming to see your people then, I presume?'

'Indeed,' I said, and we laughed.

And no, he and I were not from the same clan. He was a Sinclair.

He was travelling to see his granddaughter, who had just had a baby.

'You got any children?'

'No, I'm without offspring. Motherhood is not my destined role, I'm afraid.'

'I'm terribly sorry,' he said, staring out the window momentarily, trying to organise his thoughts. 'There's no need to reproduce all the time. You know, it is here that Charles Darwin came unstuck. Altruistic ants make nonsense of the theory of natural selection and "survival of the fittest".

As Darwin found out, ants are not in competition but are so cooperative so much that worker ants sacrifice their reproductive ambitions. According to Darwin, they have zero fitness and should be long extinct. Yet, there they are making bright and beautiful appearances every spring, in every ant generation.'

'I'm not religious.'

'I'm speaking of evolution, my dear, not religion.'

'I don't know enough about Darwin, but what you said sounds incomplete.'

We disagreed without being disagreeable.

When we arrived in Inverness, I helped him carry his bags to the taxi rank, and we said bye.

I walked to the car hire company and drove off with a basic budget car suitable for my shallow pockets.

The drive to the Hebrides was like taking a slip road into another dimension. Fluffy little clouds flung so high across the heavens. The mountains reminded me of the Eastern Highlands of Zimbabwe.

I had not warned George that I was coming. If George could vanish just like that, that selfishly, George had forfeited any right to be warned.

George earned pocket money by picking up French and German tourists from Inverness and driving them to the Western Isles. The hustle was only viable if one took advantage of the ferry ticket discount for farmers transporting livestock. I had looked at George's little website, through which bookings could be made. Comments were permanently disabled. That is not a good look, George.

I checked in at a hotel in Stornoway, gathered my thoughts

and lines, and then found the courage to call George's home number.

'Hello?' It was a subdued voice.

'Is George around?'

'Sorry, wrong number.' The line went dead.

Maybe George was no longer George?

I called the number again. Someone lifted the receiver and said nothing. I could hear soft breathing. I listened, locked into pulsing silence with the person at the other end. Then the line went dead.

On the drive back to Inverness, I didn't listen to any music. I preferred the sound of the engine.

36

When I return from Scotland, I go out clubbing for five nights in a row, looking for familiar heartbeats in the crowd. On the fifth night I stumble out into the streets at 3 a.m. and run into a flash mob on Old Street. Everyone is merry, in good spirits; it's the curious hour when people are semi-religious, are at the peak of their hope that light is about to appear and scatter their twenty-first-century kind of despair. I must join them.

An hour later, the mob has turned into a search party and we're looking for a vulnerable woman who vanished into a dark alley. We look high and low, and the crowd begins to disintegrate as people go in different directions now that someone has created a Telegram Messenger group to co-ordinate the search.

I must peel off. I'm tired of looking for the woman and I need some sleep.

I get home and look at my Telegram. I find someone has shared a picture of the missing woman, and there I am, in a hoodie. Even I do not recognise myself at first; with the hoodie down, the search party could not hope to identify me.

I pull myself together and prepare to sail through the years, compact in spirit as one can be, with neither hope nor despair. I was never going to hear from George.

When I return to Brighton for the first time to see Nishta and Gabriel, I take two terrariums in bell jar vessels.

I had tried last month to arrange to meet Nishta first, one weekend, and Gabriel the next, but something came up in Gabriel's work life. Now I have to fit in both on the same day. They live at opposite ends of the city.

Brighton train station has not changed one bit. I can't help walking past Lost & Found to see if I recognise anyone. A disinterested young man scrolling through a smartphone. Sitting next to him is a wiry old woman. I remember her. She tried to help me after Nishta and Gabriel dropped me at the station ten years ago. She looks exhausted by this gig; the years and routine show on her face.

I remember after Nishta and Gabriel left, I went straight to platform 5, where my bobble hat was blown off my head by a gust, flew away and landed on the tracks. That now tired-looking lady came to me in a hi-vis vest shaking a walkie-talkie at the hat. Said my hat would be retrieved at midnight but that I should only expect to have it back if it was made of lead otherwise it'll be halfway to London by midnight.

I take the long route past the Cinque Terre café, where George and I once waitressed. The owner has changed the

161

café's name to The Honest Italian. Gabriel has dabbled in politics and stood as a populist candidate, telling people there were too many foreigners in the country. He is a high flyer after reinventing himself with the help of an old schoolmate. The diversity, equality and inclusion industry managers woke up to Gabriel's charms and decided he was one of them. Now Gabriel attends meetings in Downing Street, meetings that cannot be interrupted by phone calls except in the run-up to elections when a call from a Hollywood star, the Dalai Lama, Peppa Pig's producer or a splayed-out Nazi that everyone politely pretends is just clowning is gold dust for a government that has nothing to offer but the same.

'Shamiso, it's perfect!' Nishta says about the terrarium.

'I made it in a workshop at the local plant nursery.'

'You're so thoughtful. I read about terrariums but never got around to making one. This is beautiful.'

Nishta makes lunch from a quiche that she made and froze at the beginning of the week.

'You have not changed in years, in looks or habits,' I laugh.

'And have you changed, Shamiso?'

We sit to eat. She is a happy divorcee.

'Still can't get a good dinner table anecdote out of the whole thing. Yes, there was violence, the psychological variety. And there was qualified redemption but no miracles. Now, what about you?'

'I have no news. Nothing new to share except that I am now in the second phase of my self-discovery. Does that match your brevity?'

162

'Self-discovery? Are you into New Age poppycock now?'

'When did you become so narrow?'

'Are you and George in touch?'

'George never replied to my letter and would not take my call last time I tried.'

Nishta smiles.

'Is there something I don't know?'

'I have another cat for you, if you want her.' Nishta gestures towards the creature walking through the door. An elderly neighbour passed away, leaving the cat in Nishta's care.

'I'll take it if you promise to come see my place in London and stay at least a night.'

'I would love that. Things that you can do when you divorce. I'm sorry we couldn't visit you all these years. Gabriel worried it may hurt his ambitions if it was found he had visited an illegal and did not bother to inform the authorities.'

By the time I arrive at Gabriel's, I'm carrying a cat and a plant.

'This one is called Eva!' I say to Gabriel, who takes one look at the cat and finds he has nothing good to say about it.

But he loves his terrarium.

'This is absolutely delightful, Shamiso.'

'I thought it might brighten up your study. And don't worry about killing it; I made sure it's low maintenance.'

'Can't promise I won't kill it, I'm afraid. Not intentionally, of course.'

Gabriel gives me a look and switches on the kettle.

We talk about the general, pointless and impersonal stuff that one could read in a newspaper's op-eds. We step around each other carefully, avoiding difficult questions. Why did you leave Nishta? Why are you still an illegal?

We drink tea, and, when we have run out of false talk, Gabriel says, 'Would you be so kind as to help me with my grocery shopping down the lane?'

'How can you ask your guest to help you do your chores?'

'It's nice to have companionship while shopping on occasion. You can't say I haven't earned the privilege of benefiting from your company, can you?'

'Mercenary!'

We lock the cat in and walk to a newly built Waitrose supermarket.

Gabriel grabs the trolley, and I follow as we go through the aisles, picking stuff off the shelves. Gabriel is quick and efficient, like someone with a weekly shopping list that has not changed in a long time.

Gabriel says I must take a bottle of good wine back to London. I am still trying to process this, and the next thing I see is Gabriel shooting off in extraordinary strides, abandoning the trolley.

A few minutes later, he reappears, looking sheepish. 'I'm sorry about that.'

Gabriel spotted an old Zambian acquaintance, a comrade in the anti-apartheid movement in London. Gabriel's struggle credentials would be ruined if the man saw him in Waitrose. Cannot be seen to have joined the ranks of black people who think economic success comes before liberation.

Early that evening I catch my train back to London.

37

A letter arrives from George out of the blue, and when I read it I can hear George loudly and clearly, as though we we're in the same room.

I'm sorry it took me such a long time to reply.

At first I cannot read the rest. I need to make a cup of tea, centre myself, so I can come to the letter with the right kind of head, the correct attention.

By the time I get to the end of the letter, a switch has flicked: I understand completely what this means. I can go home now.

Of course I have always known this is what I wanted from George but had somehow conspired to conceal it from myself, perhaps as an act of self-preservation: the possibility that I was never going to hear from George would have destroyed me when I could afford neither hope nor despair. I just had to carry on, keep moving.

I sleep on the letter, thinking what to say to George now that all the loose ends are tied. Did I need to write back? Would a phone call suffice?

Babamukuru appears at my doorstep in a dream on a bright sunny day and paws a bright-coloured bug on the doormat. It spreads its wings, takes to the air, flying up and up until it has vanished into the cobalt-blue sky. There follows a throbbing silence. We wait in anticipation, and then it comes: a tremendous crash up in the heavens. After that Babamukuru steps into my flat.

Towards the end of the week I grab my phone and earphones, put my shoes on and take the long walk to the city to gather all the things I left there.

The routines and rituals that I've built over years, I will have to lay them down elsewhere again, start all over again.

Over the years I have taken long walks to the city centre, listening to a podcast. When I want to secure my thoughts, I listen to music over the length of my walk, depositing them over a five-mile walk, hanging each on what I see along the way. From a tall spire. Under a train bridge. On the roof of an underpass.

I left something about George on the Elephant & Castle roundabout. I left things on the riverbank, on a flight of pigeons and on a homeless person's tent in a park. I am coming to gather my things.

The weekly gig at the Crypt Jazz, I will miss. But the singing, I can take that with me and find a way of following Stella Chiweshe to the inner places they go to when singing 'Nhemamusasa', speaking from inside the mbira's acoustic orb when it begins to compel the gathered to clap the night to pieces for the return of the River God.

Acknowledgements

Thanks and acknowledgements to Arts Council England, the Society of Authors, the Dora Maar House, the Santa Maddalena Foundation, Civitella Ranieri, Villa Marguerite Yourcenar, Cove Park and the Stellenbosch Institute for Advanced Study.